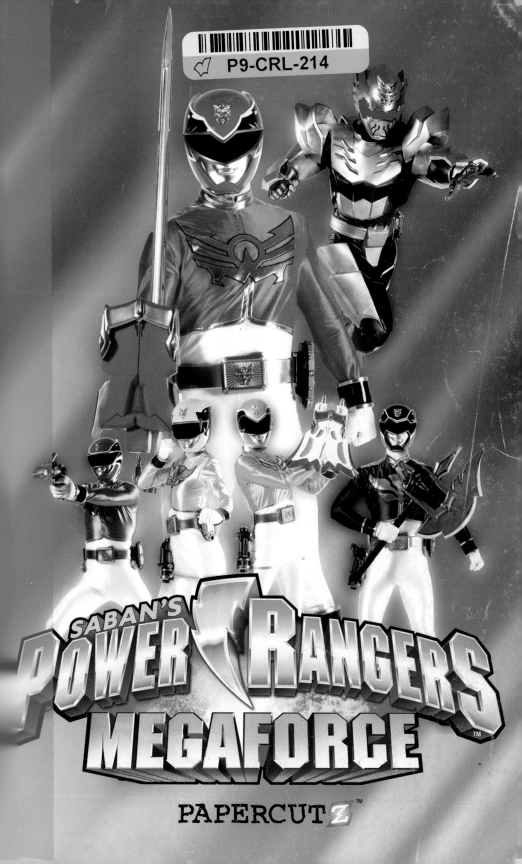

SABAN'S
POWER RANGERS
MEGAFORCE

PAPERCUT Z™

SABAN'S POWER RANGERS™

Graphic Novels Available From PAPERCUTZ™

1 "MEMORY SHORT"
SABAN'S POWER RANGERS
SUPER SAMURAI
Stefan Petrucha
Paulo Henrique
PAPERCUTZ

Graphic Novel #1

2 "TERRIBLE TOYS"
Stefan Petrucha • Paulo Henrique
SABAN'S POWER RANGERS
SUPER SAMURAI
PAPERCUTZ

Graphic Novel #2

3 "PANIC IN THE PARADE"
Stefan Petrucha • PH Marcondes
SABAN'S POWER RANGERS
MEGAFORCE
PLUS: THE BLACK RANGER vs VRAK in
"GAME ON!"
PAPERCUTZ

Graphic Novel #3

4 "BROKEN WORLD"
Stefan Petrucha • PH Marcondes
SABAN'S POWER RANGERS
MEGAFORCE
PAPERCUTZ

Coming Soon: Graphic Novel #4

POWER RANGERS graphic novels are available for $6.99 each in paperback, and $10.99 in hardcover. Available from booksellers everywhere. You can also order online from papercutz.com. Or call 1-800-886-1223, Monday through Friday, 9 – 5 EST. MC, Visa, and AmEx accepted. To order by mail, please add $4.00 for postage and handling for first book ordered, $1.00 for each additional book and make check payable to NBM Publishing. Send to: Papercutz, 160 Broadway, Suite 700, East Wing, New York, NY 10038.

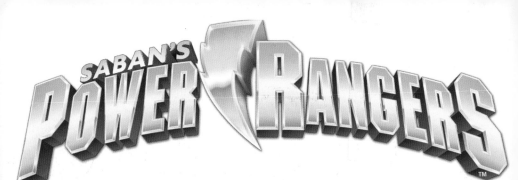

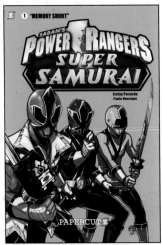

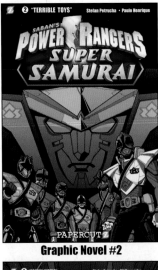

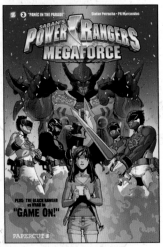

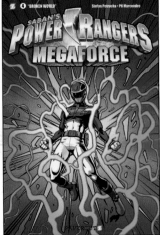

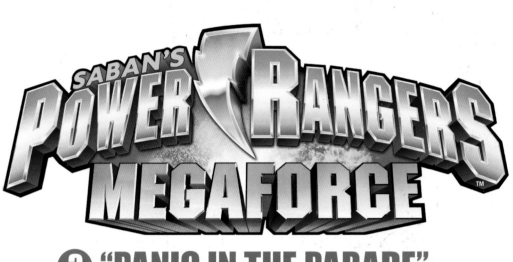

SABAN'S POWER RANGERS MEGAFORCE™

3 "PANIC IN THE PARADE"

Stefan Petrucha – Writer
PH Marcondes – Artist
Laurie E. Smith and Mindy Indy– Colorists

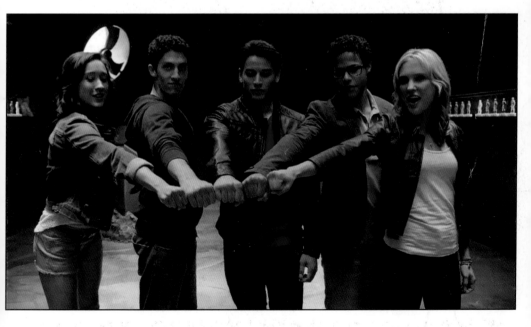

PAPERCUTZ™
New York

SABAN'S POWER RANGERS MEGAFORCE
#3 "PANIC IN THE PARADE"

"Panic in the Parade"
STEFAN PETRUCHA -- Writer
PH MARCONDES -- Artist
MINDY INDY -- Colorist
BRYAN SENKA -- Letterer

"Game On!"
STEFAN PETRUCHA -- Writer
PH MARCONDES -- Artist
LAURIE E. SMITH -- Colorist
BRYAN SENKA -- Letterer

UMESH PATEL (RangerCrew) -- Special Thanks
KAY OLIVER and MARY RAFFERTY -- Extra Special Thanks
JESSE POST -- Marketing Director
BETH SCORZATO -- Production Coordinator
MICHAEL PETRANEK -- Editor
JIM SALICRUP
Editor-in-Chief

ISBN: 978-1-59707-351-6 paperback edition
ISBN: 978-1-59707-352-3 hardcover edition

Printed in China
July 2013 by O.G. Printing Productions, LTD.
Units 2&3, 5/F, Lemmi Centre
50 Hoi Yuen Road
Kwong Tong, Kowloon

Papercutz books may be purchased for business or promotional use. For information on bulk purchases please contact
Macmillan Corporate and Premium Sales Department at (800) 221-7945 x5442.

Distributed by Macmillan

First Printing

MEET SABAN'S POWER RANGERS MEGAFORCE™

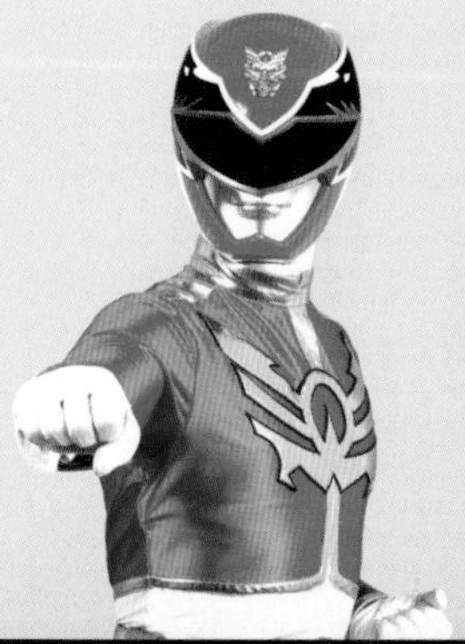

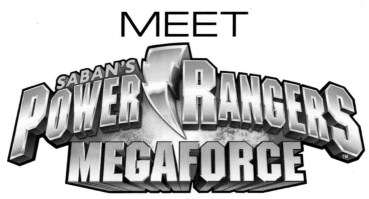

For centuries, the Earth has been protected by a supernatural guardian being named Gosei and his robotic aide, Tensou. When the evil Warstar aliens begin their massive invasion, Gosei calls upon five teenagers to form the ultimate team... the Power Rangers Megaforce!

Using their newfound abilities, mega-weapons, tech Zords and Megazords, the fate of the world rests in the hands of the Power Rangers Megaforce.

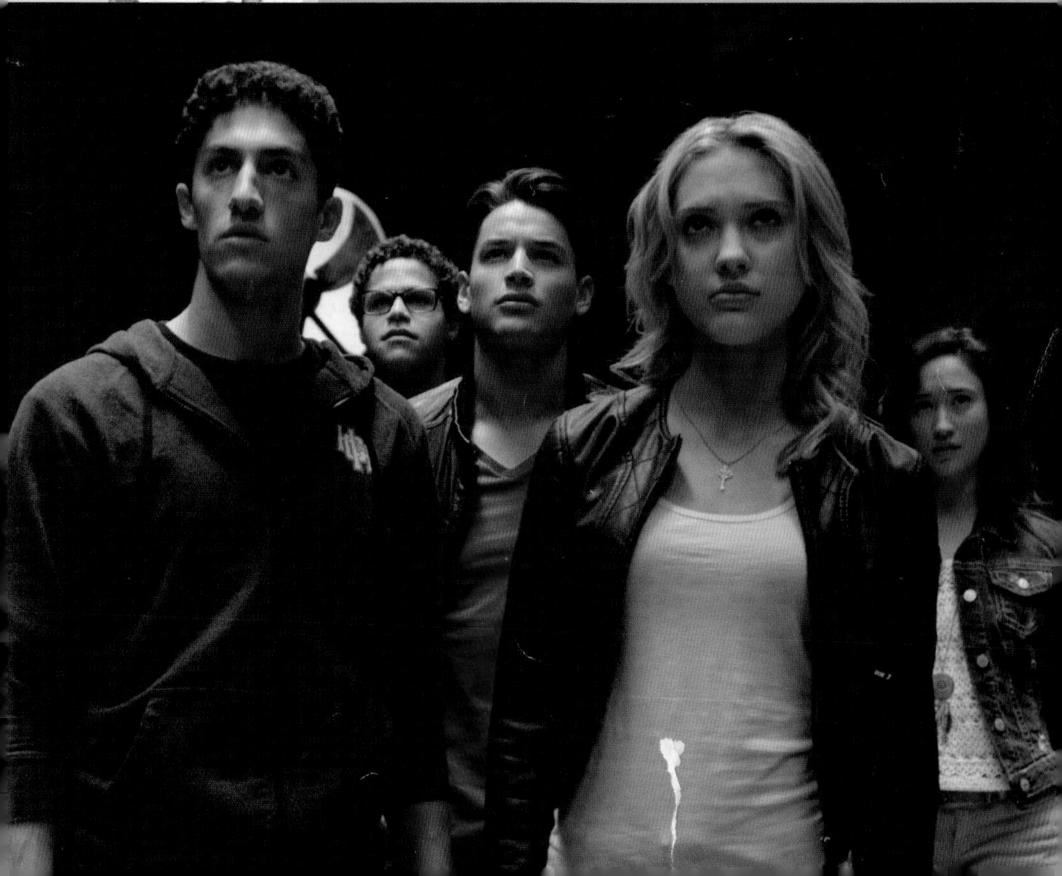

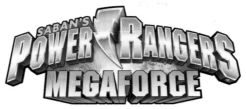

THE RED RANGER (TROY BURROWS)

Troy finds himself as the new kid in town... again. Moving often has made Troy grow up fast, as he had to quickly learn how to take care of himself. Troy is a bit of a loner, but he's eager to make friends in his new hometown. His life, however, is about to take an unexpected turn.

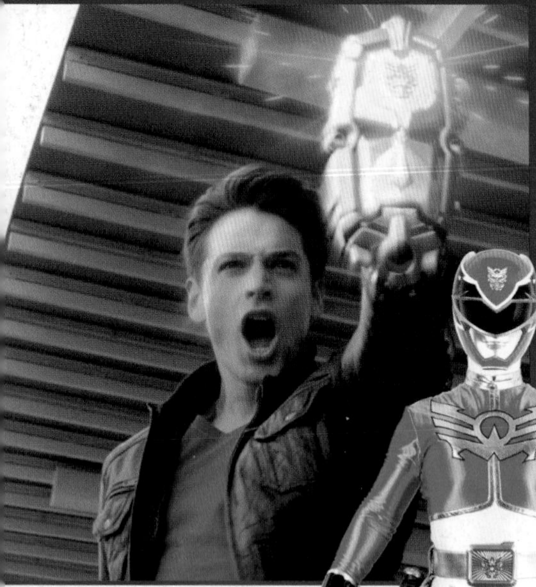

Troy enjoys practicing and perfecting his martial arts skills. He's got the focus and discipline to make him a force to be reckoned with. He doesn't look for trouble but he'll never run from it when someone is in need. Compassionate and loyal, Troy is a champion of the underdog be they human or alien.

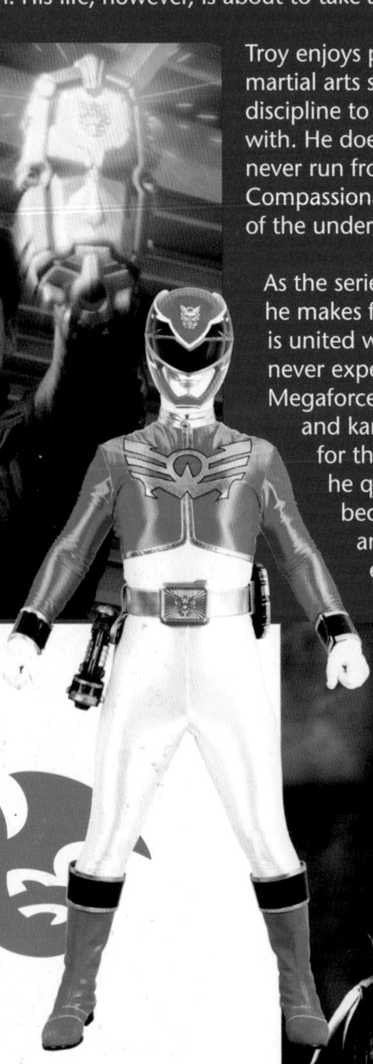

As the series begins, Troy is grateful when he makes friends with the other teens and is united with them as the Megaforce. Troy never expected to be the leader of the Megaforce, but with his manner, discipline, and karate skills, it's as if he were training for the job all his life. A natural leader, he quickly rises to the challenge of becoming the newest Red Ranger and leading his comrades into every skirmish with courage and determination.

Weapon:
Dragon Sword

Elemental Power:
Sky

Zord:
Dragon

Signature Move:
Sky Dragon

Notes:
It's his destiny to lead the Megaforce.

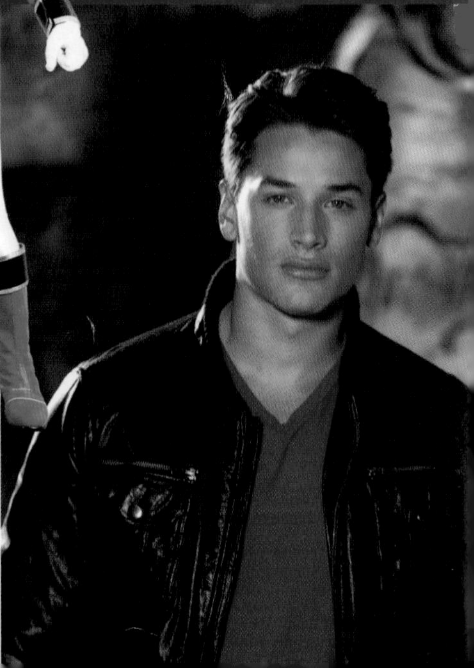

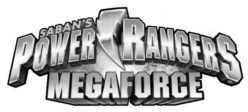

THE PINK RANGER (EMMA GOODALL)

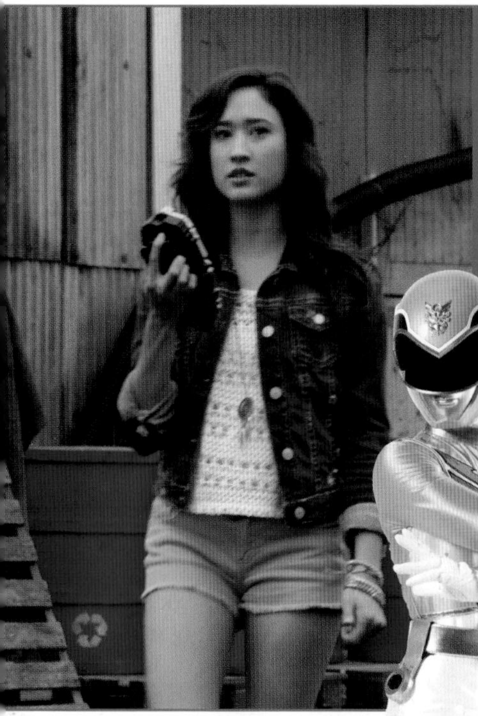

Emma is a compassionate and charitable teen who will do what it takes to protect the environment. While photography is a great way for Emma to express her love of nature, her more wild side has a desire to be a BMX biker.

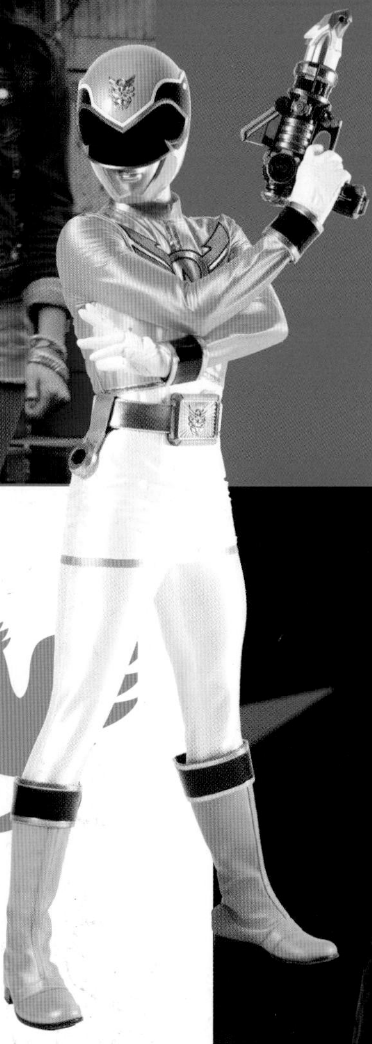

Surprised like the rest of the Ranger team when called upon to be part of the Megaforce, Emma takes the alien attacks on the environment personally and is anxious to protect the world. As the Pink Ranger, not only is it Emma's goal to save the world, but to make it a better place.

Weapon:
Phoenix Flare

Elemental Power:
Sky

Zord:
Phoenix

Signature Move:
Air Phoenix

Notes:
Emma is a skilled BMX cyclist.

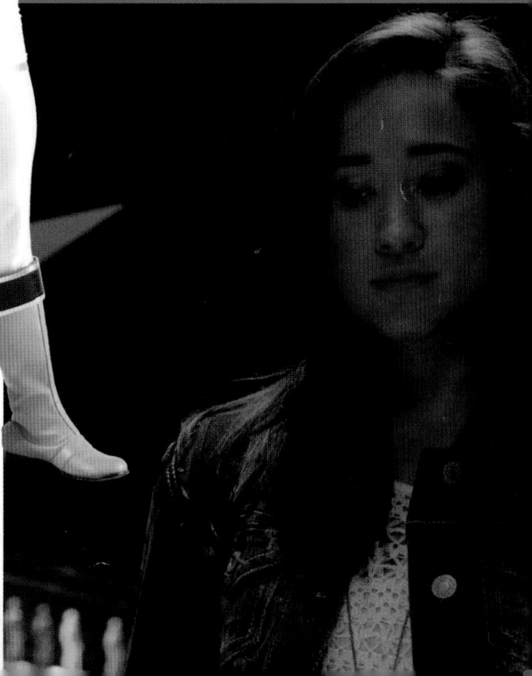

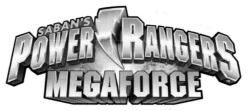

THE BLUE RANGER (NOAH CARVER)

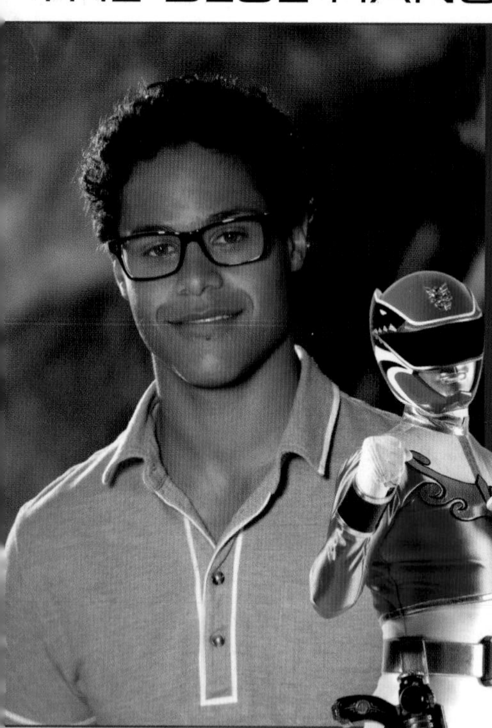

The school's geek, Noah is incredibly clever and kind, but a bit socially akward. He often finds himself dragged into social adventures by Jake, the Black Ranger, when he would rather remain safely in the warm glow of a computer monitor. He has an insatiable thirst for knowledge and is awed by the fact that aliens are attacking the Earth. Since becoming a Ranger, he is even more excited by the technology that the team gets to use in their battles.

The combination of Jake's social savvy and Noah's tech skills make them a great team. The physical part of being a Power Ranger is the hardest part for Noah but with Troy and Jake being at his side, they encourage him to try. In the end, Noah succeeds by employing his true strength-- brainpower Noah shares his love of science and the paranormal with his goofy sciene teacher, Mr. Burley.

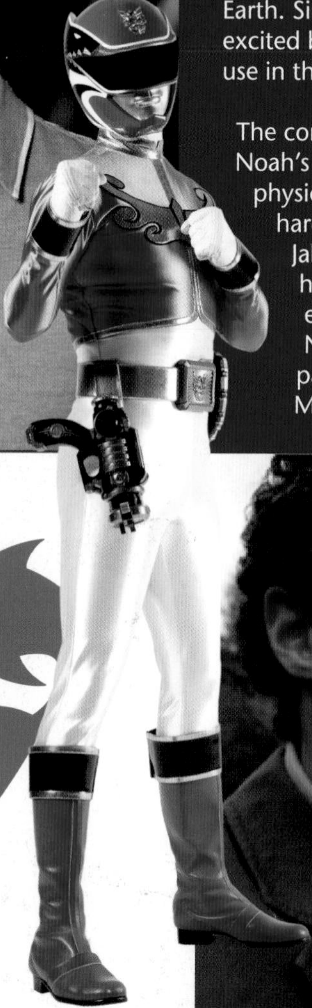

Weapon:
Shark bow

Element:
Sea

Zord:
Shark

Notes:
Noah shares his love of the paranormal with his science teacher, Mr. Burley.

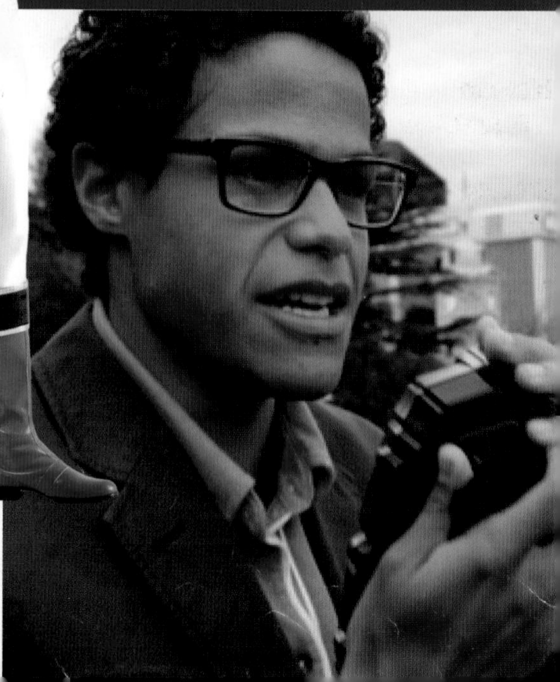

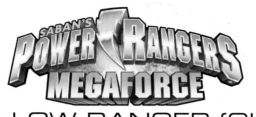

THE YELLOW RANGER (GIA MORAN)

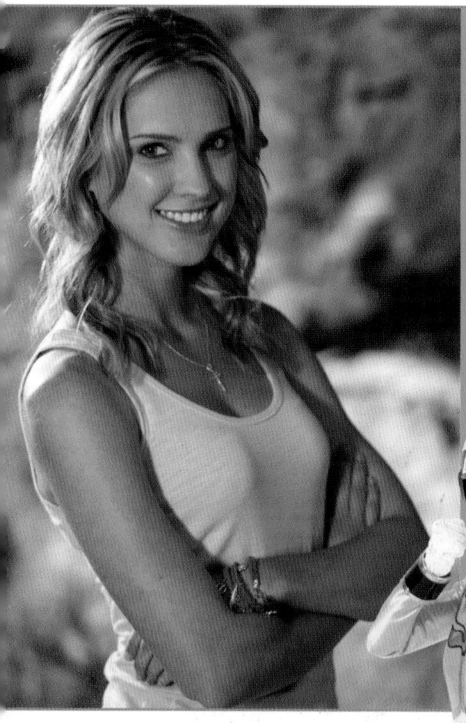

Gia is beautiful, smart and a formidable martial artist with a generally unflappable demeanor. Not only is she the prettiest and most intelligent girl at school, she is also the toughest. While her personable manner tempts many boys, her martial art skills keep them at bay. Gia carries herself with a sense of confidence that comes from success.

She is loyal to her friends and is best friends with Emma, the Pink Ranger. They have known each other since they were little girls and have remained friends even though they are now very different.

Gia is the perfect addition to the Power Rangers team even though at times her effortless success furstrates her new teammates, but everyone knows they can count on her.

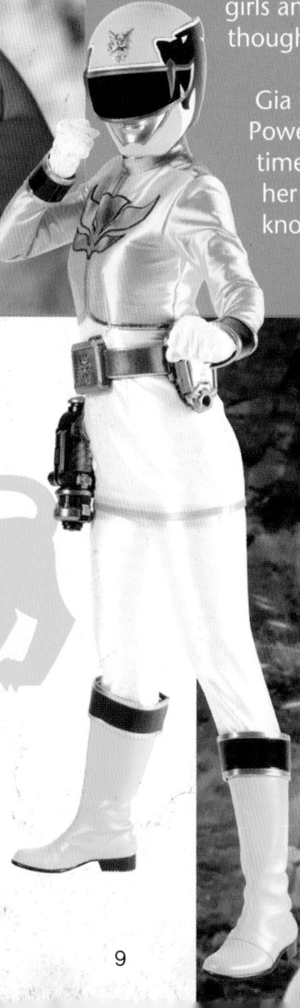

Weapon:
Tiger Claw

Element:
Earth

Zord:
Tiger

Notes:
Jake (the Black Ranger) has a crush on her.

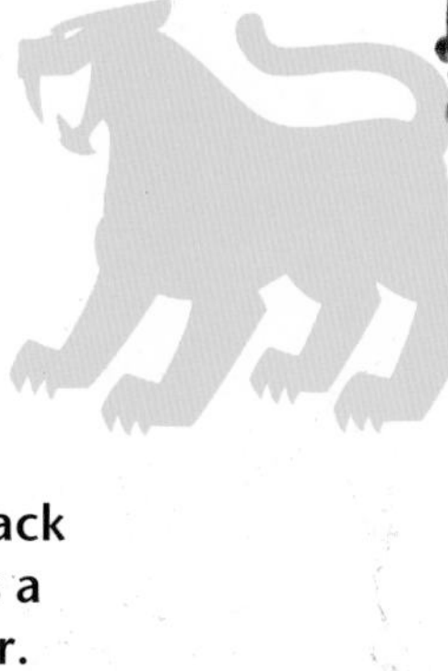

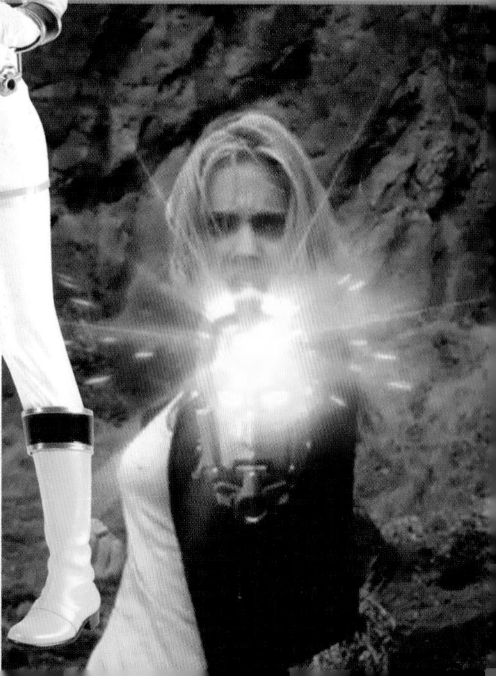

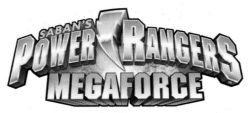

THE BLACK RANGER (JAKE HOLLING

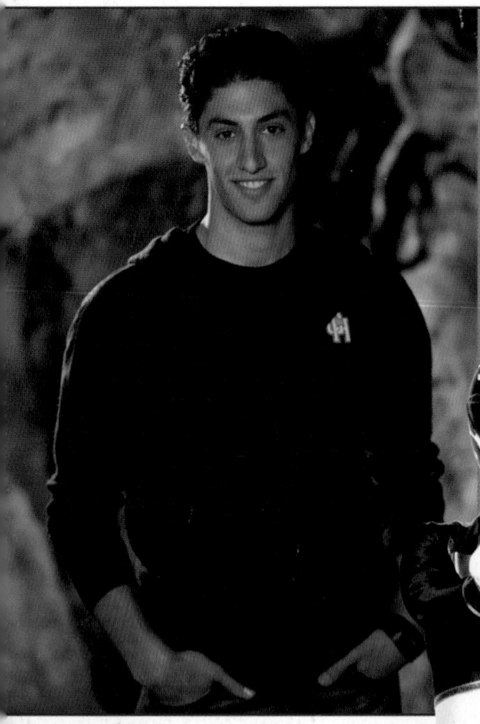

Jake is a fearless, fun-loving teen with a never-ending well of optimism. His athletic abilities are good enough to make the team, but not be the star player. His main passion in life is soccer and it's rare to find him without a soccer ball nearby. Jake's fearlessness also applies to his social life. His determination will not allow something like the lack of an invitation to stop him from going to a party or getting out on the dance floor.

He is best friends with Noah, the Blue Ranger, whom he never stops trying to get to loosen up and have some fun. Jake sees his new super-hero role as an opportunity to do great things even if he occasionally wishes he could let the world know that he's the one saving it. Jake does have one major weak spot and that's his crush on Gia, the Yellow Ranger. He tries to play things cool but he wears his heart on his sleeve and he's certain that one day he'll win her over.

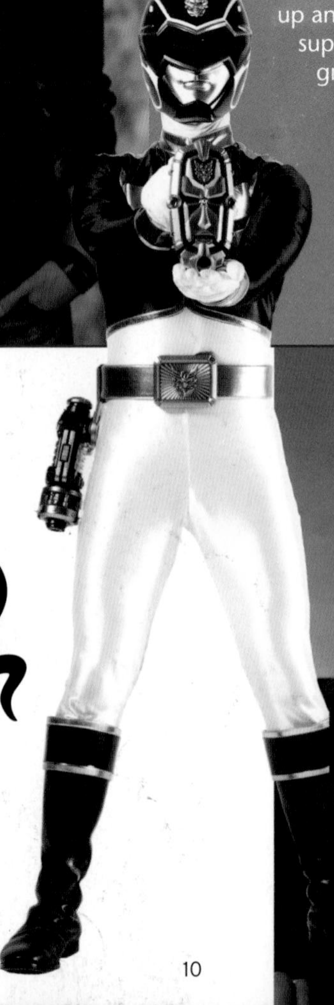

Weapon:
Snake Axe

Elemental Power:
Earth

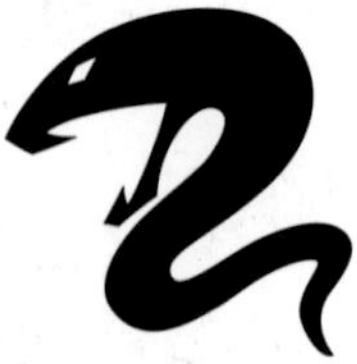

Zord:
Snake

Notes:
Jake is an excellent soccer player, and often has a ball with him.

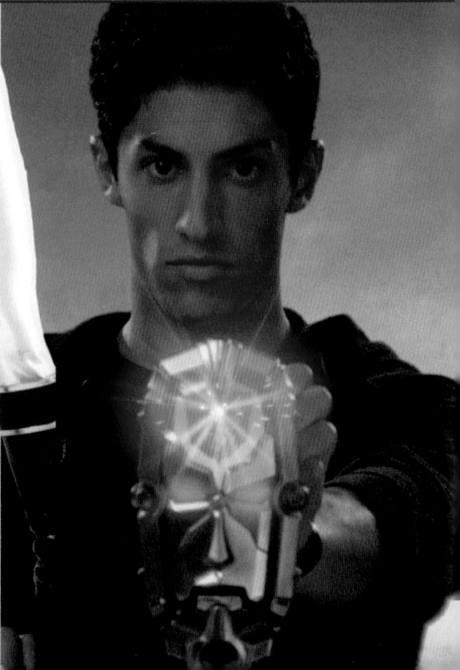

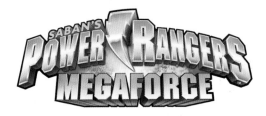

ROBO KNIGHT

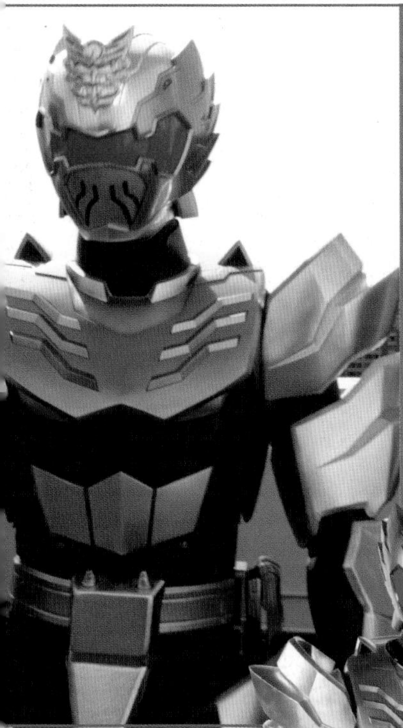

When the Rangers are in the battle for their lives, suddenly there appears an unknown Ranger wearing the same Gosei symbol. The Rangers instantly know he is a part of the Power Rangers. Robo Knight was created by Gosei centuries ago to protect the Earth at all costs. He is powered by the Earth's own elements and he can call on those same elements to use as his powers.

Robo Knight, however, had been buried for centuries and only recently awakened when the Earth sensed danger. The long sleep affected many portions of his memory and now there are times he sees humans as the greatest threat to the Earth. The Power Rangers slowly remind him that there are great attributes to be human and that the Power Rangers see Robo Knight as a good friend-- something he had long forgotten. Unlike the Rangers who have to call their Zords, Robo Knight has the unique ability to morph into his Lion Zord and back again to a robot. A power the Rangers witness firsthand.

Robo Knight learns that humanity's fate is intertwined with Earth's and both are worth saving.

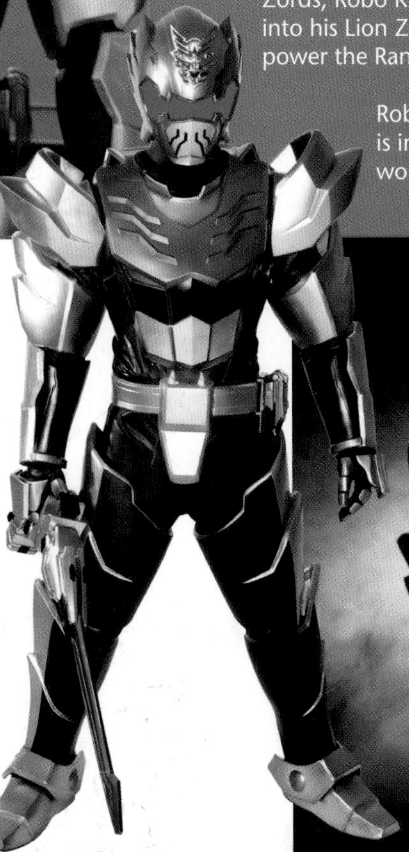

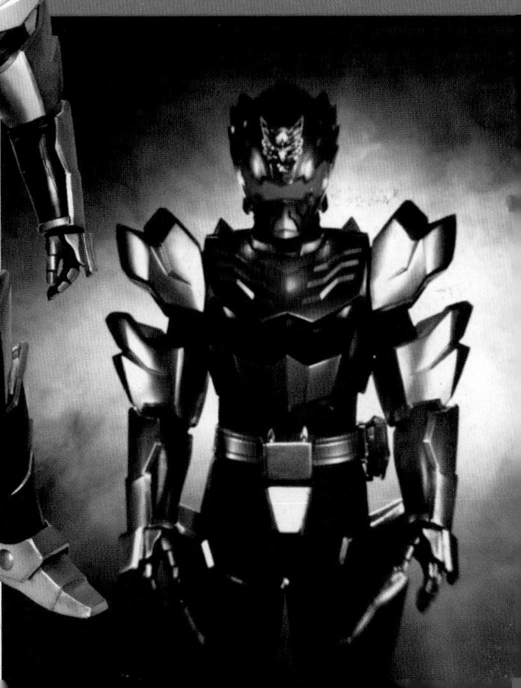

Weapon:
Robo Blaster and Robo Blade

Element:
Access to all Elemental Powers

Zord:
Lion

Notes:
He is the defacto sixth ranger.

ADMIRAL MALKOR

Admiral Malkor is the moth-like commander of the Warstar ship, and the leader of the alien attack force. His goal is to make the Insectoids rule the Earth, and for humans to be nothing but a distant memory. He does not tolerate failure.

VRAK

Vrak is not an Insectoid-- he is a member of the alien royal family, and brother to the prince who commands the imminent invasion. He is unique with special powers not possessed by the Insectoids, and seeks to one day use his intelligence to rule over the other aliens, and become emperor.

CREEPOX

The hulking Insectoid lieutenant that serves at Malkor's side, Creepox, believes firmly in insect superiority. He would like nothing more than to unleash a full-scale attack on planet Earth, and is obsessed with defeating the Red Ranger in one-on-one combat.

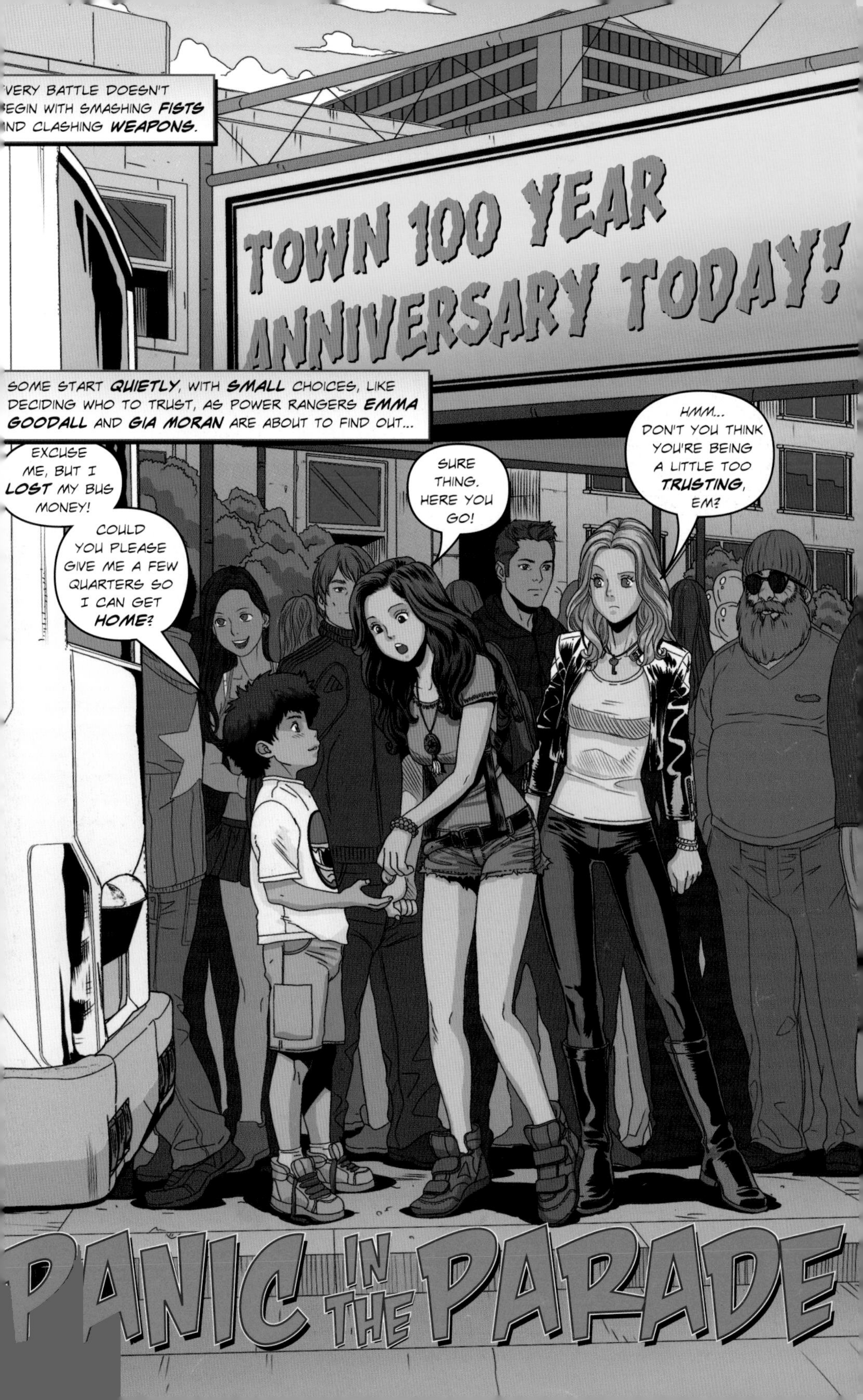

EVERY BATTLE DOESN'T BEGIN WITH SMASHING **FISTS** AND CLASHING **WEAPONS.**
TOWN 100 YEAR ANNIVERSARY TODAY!
SOME START **QUIETLY**, WITH **SMALL** CHOICES, LIKE DECIDING WHO TO TRUST, AS POWER RANGERS **EMMA GOODALL** AND **GIA MORAN** ARE ABOUT TO FIND OUT...
EXCUSE ME, BUT I **LOST** MY BUS MONEY!
COULD YOU PLEASE GIVE ME A FEW QUARTERS SO I CAN GET **HOME?**
SURE THING. HERE YOU GO!
HMM... DON'T YOU THINK YOU'RE BEING A LITTLE TOO **TRUSTING**, EM?
PANIC IN THE PARADE

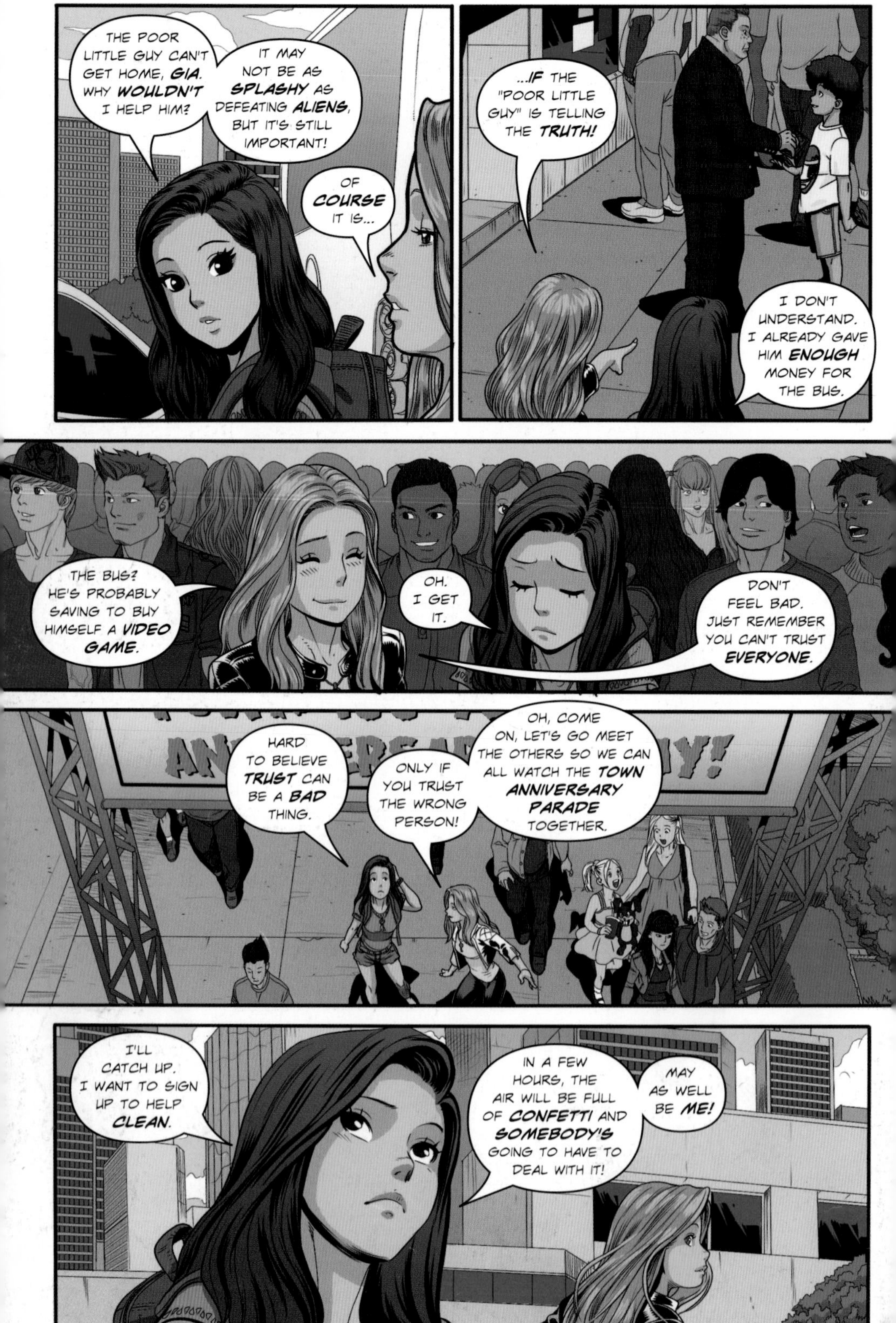

THE POOR LITTLE GUY CAN'T GET HOME, GIA. WHY WOULDN'T I HELP HIM?
IT MAY NOT BE AS SPLASHY AS DEFEATING ALIENS, BUT IT'S STILL IMPORTANT!
OF COURSE IT IS...
...IF THE "POOR LITTLE GUY" IS TELLING THE TRUTH!
I DON'T UNDERSTAND. I ALREADY GAVE HIM ENOUGH MONEY FOR THE BUS.
THE BUS? HE'S PROBABLY SAVING TO BUY HIMSELF A VIDEO GAME.
OH. I GET IT.
DON'T FEEL BAD. JUST REMEMBER YOU CAN'T TRUST EVERYONE.
HARD TO BELIEVE TRUST CAN BE A BAD THING.
ONLY IF YOU TRUST THE WRONG PERSON!
OH, COME ON, LET'S GO MEET THE OTHERS SO WE CAN ALL WATCH THE TOWN ANNIVERSARY PARADE TOGETHER.
I'LL CATCH UP. I WANT TO SIGN UP TO HELP CLEAN.
IN A FEW HOURS, THE AIR WILL BE FULL OF CONFETTI AND SOMEBODY'S GOING TO HAVE TO DEAL WITH IT!
MAY AS WELL BE ME!

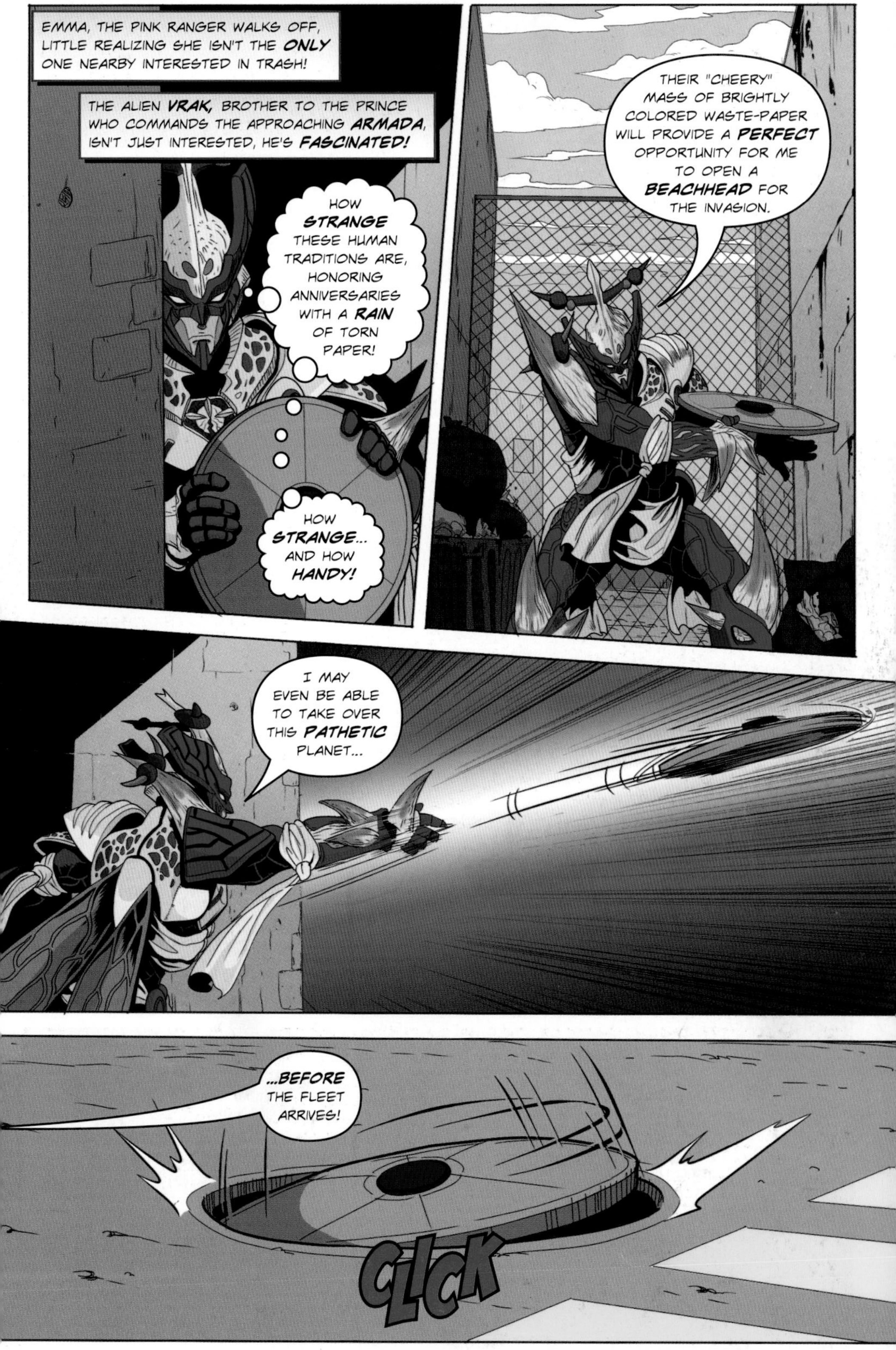
EMMA, THE PINK RANGER WALKS OFF, LITTLE REALIZING SHE ISN'T THE ONLY ONE NEARBY INTERESTED IN TRASH!
THE ALIEN VRAK, BROTHER TO THE PRINCE WHO COMMANDS THE APPROACHING ARMADA, ISN'T JUST INTERESTED, HE'S FASCINATED!
HOW STRANGE THESE HUMAN TRADITIONS ARE, HONORING ANNIVERSARIES WITH A RAIN OF TORN PAPER!
HOW STRANGE... AND HOW HANDY!
THEIR "CHEERY" MASS OF BRIGHTLY COLORED WASTE-PAPER WILL PROVIDE A PERFECT OPPORTUNITY FOR ME TO OPEN A BEACHHEAD FOR THE INVASION.
I MAY EVEN BE ABLE TO TAKE OVER THIS PATHETIC PLANET...
...BEFORE THE FLEET ARRIVES!
CLICK

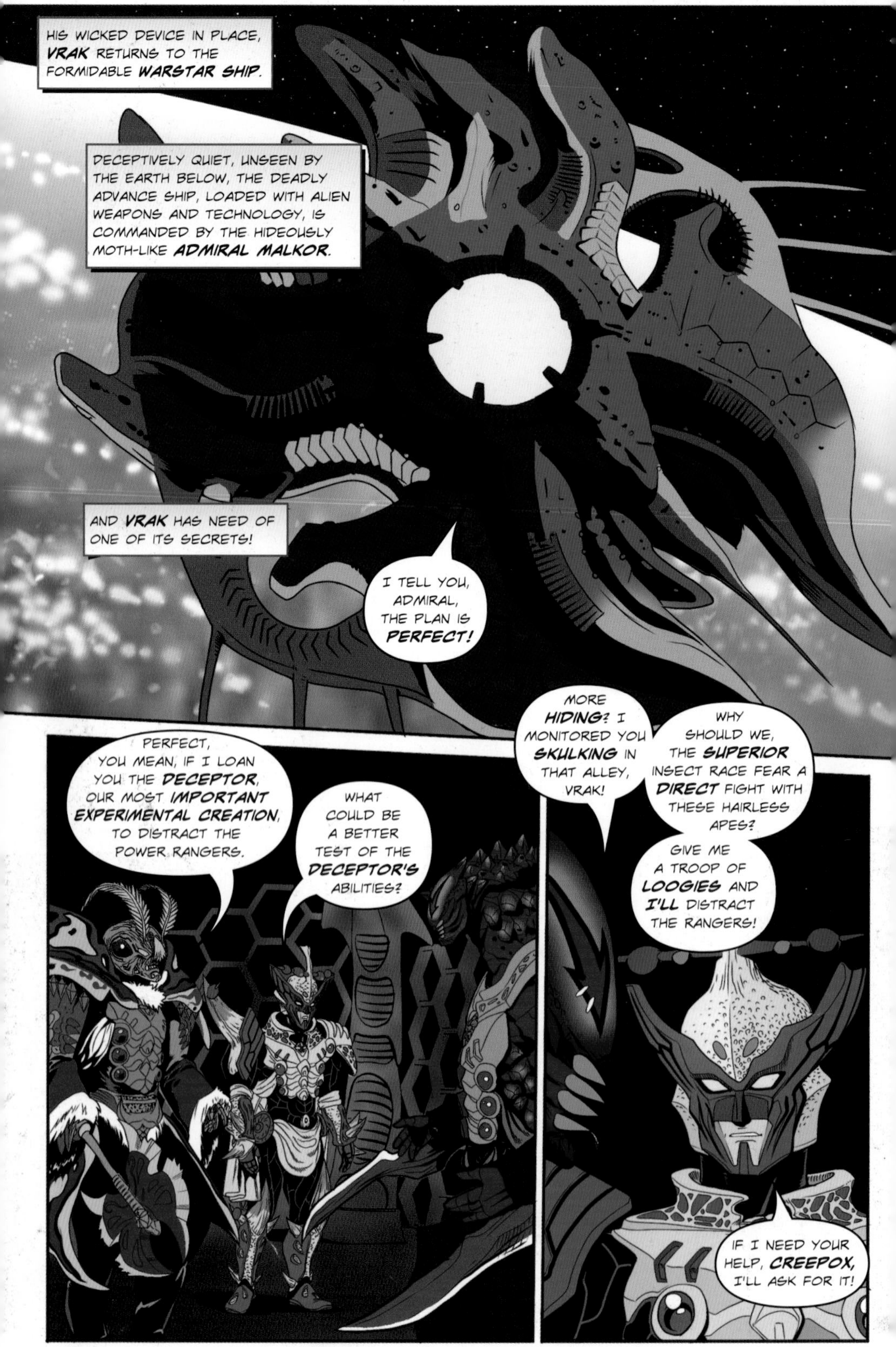
HIS WICKED DEVICE IN PLACE, VRAK RETURNS TO THE FORMIDABLE WARSTAR SHIP.
DECEPTIVELY QUIET, UNSEEN BY THE EARTH BELOW, THE DEADLY ADVANCE SHIP, LOADED WITH ALIEN WEAPONS AND TECHNOLOGY, IS COMMANDED BY THE HIDEOUSLY MOTH-LIKE ADMIRAL MALKOR.
AND VRAK HAS NEED OF ONE OF ITS SECRETS!
I TELL YOU, ADMIRAL, THE PLAN IS PERFECT!
PERFECT, YOU MEAN, IF I LOAN YOU THE DECEPTOR, OUR MOST IMPORTANT EXPERIMENTAL CREATION, TO DISTRACT THE POWER RANGERS.
WHAT COULD BE A BETTER TEST OF THE DECEPTOR'S ABILITIES?
MORE HIDING? I MONITORED YOU SKULKING IN THAT ALLEY, VRAK!
WHY SHOULD WE, THE SUPERIOR INSECT RACE FEAR A DIRECT FIGHT WITH THESE HAIRLESS APES?
GIVE ME A TROOP OF LOOGIES AND I'LL DISTRACT THE RANGERS!
IF I NEED YOUR HELP, CREEPOX, I'LL ASK FOR IT!

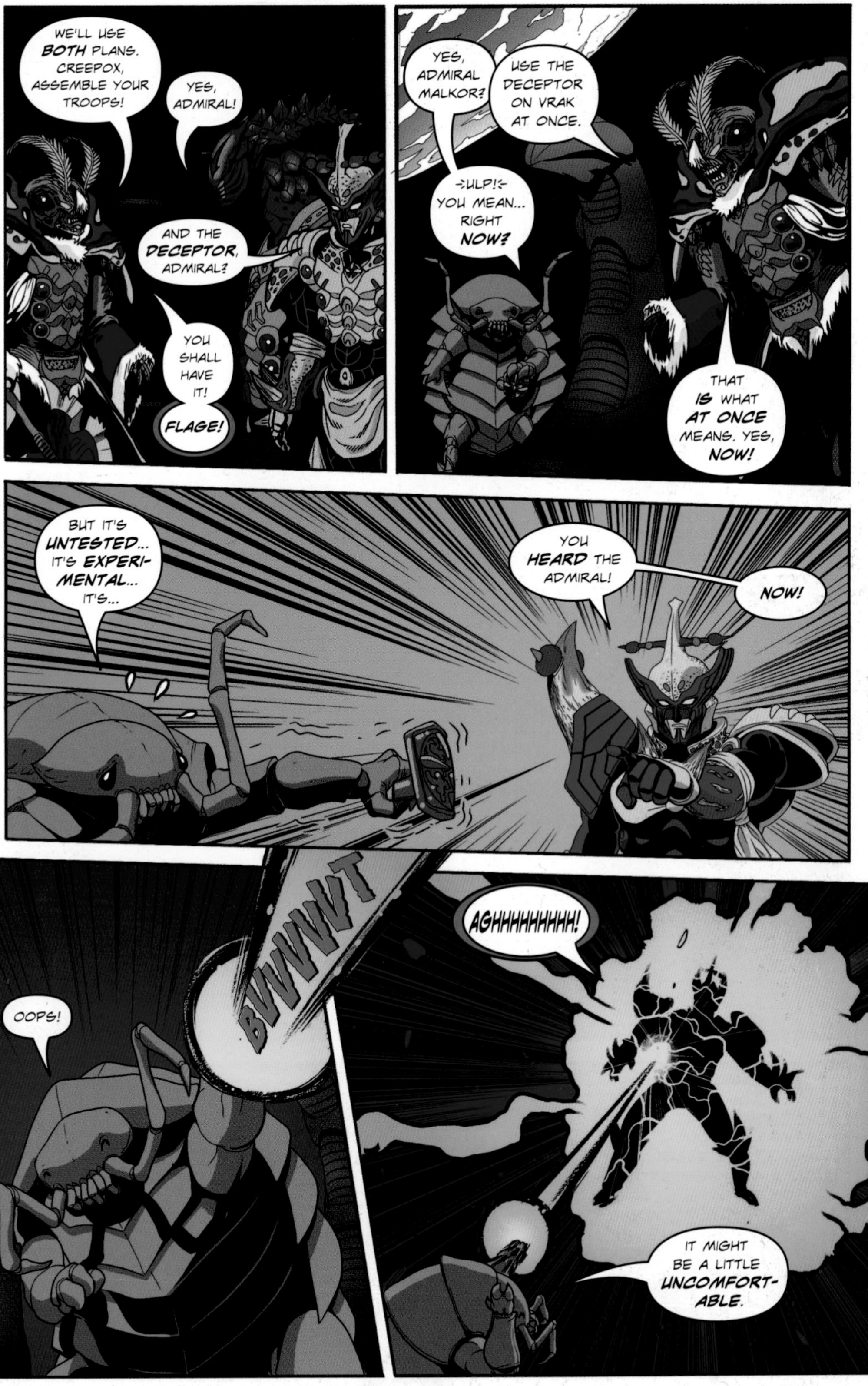
WE'LL USE BOTH PLANS. CREEPOX, ASSEMBLE YOUR TROOPS!
YES, ADMIRAL!
AND THE DECEPTOR, ADMIRAL?
YOU SHALL HAVE IT!
FLAGE!
YES, ADMIRAL MALKOR?
USE THE DECEPTOR ON VRAK AT ONCE.
-ULP!- YOU MEAN... RIGHT NOW?
THAT IS WHAT AT ONCE MEANS. YES, NOW!
BUT IT'S UNTESTED... IT'S EXPERI-MENTAL... IT'S...
YOU HEARD THE ADMIRAL!
NOW!
BVVVVVT
OOPS!
AGHHHHHHHHH!
IT MIGHT BE A LITTLE UNCOMFORT-ABLE.

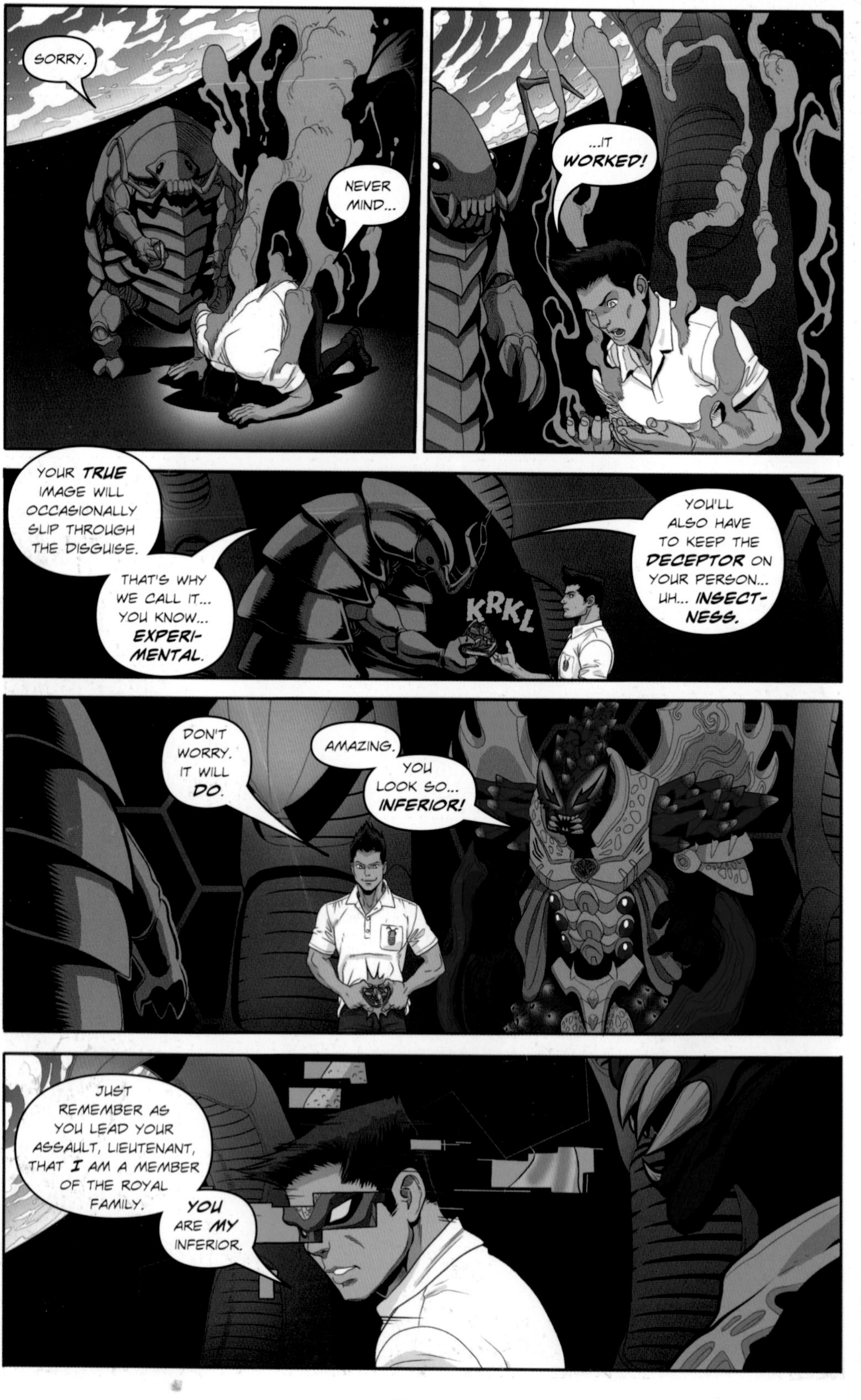
SORRY.
NEVER MIND...
...IT WORKED!
YOUR TRUE IMAGE WILL OCCASIONALLY SLIP THROUGH THE DISGUISE.
THAT'S WHY WE CALL IT... YOU KNOW... EXPERI-MENTAL.
KRKL
YOU'LL ALSO HAVE TO KEEP THE DECEPTOR ON YOUR PERSON... UH... INSECT-NESS.
DON'T WORRY. IT WILL DO.
AMAZING.
YOU LOOK SO... INFERIOR!
JUST REMEMBER AS YOU LEAD YOUR ASSAULT, LIEUTENANT, THAT I AM A MEMBER OF THE ROYAL FAMILY.
YOU ARE MY INFERIOR.

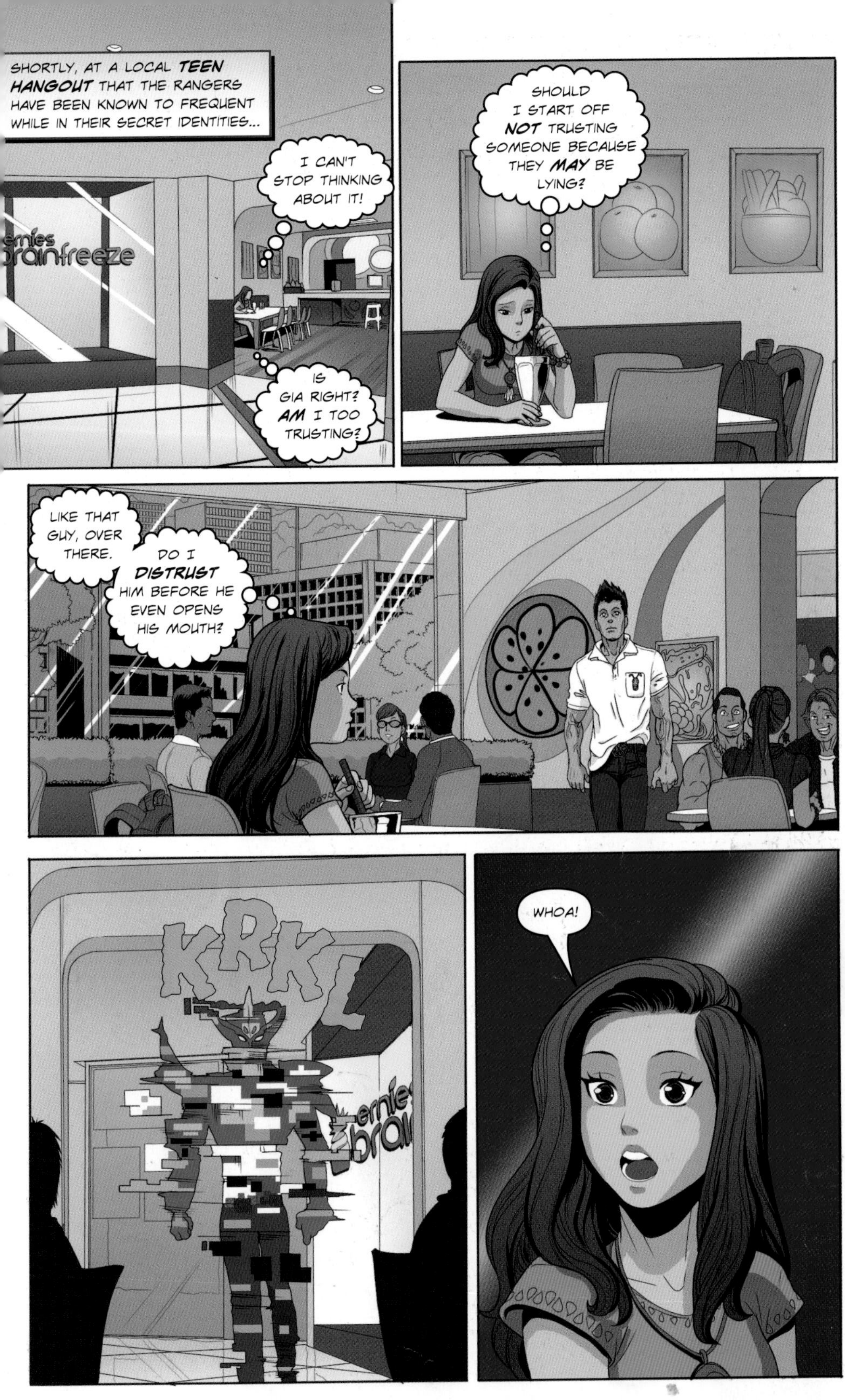
SHORTLY, AT A LOCAL TEEN HANGOUT THAT THE RANGERS HAVE BEEN KNOWN TO FREQUENT WHILE IN THEIR SECRET IDENTITIES...
I CAN'T STOP THINKING ABOUT IT!
IS GIA RIGHT? AM I TOO TRUSTING?
SHOULD I START OFF NOT TRUSTING SOMEONE BECAUSE THEY MAY BE LYING?
LIKE THAT GUY, OVER THERE.
DO I DISTRUST HIM BEFORE HE EVEN OPENS HIS MOUTH?
KRKL
WHOA!

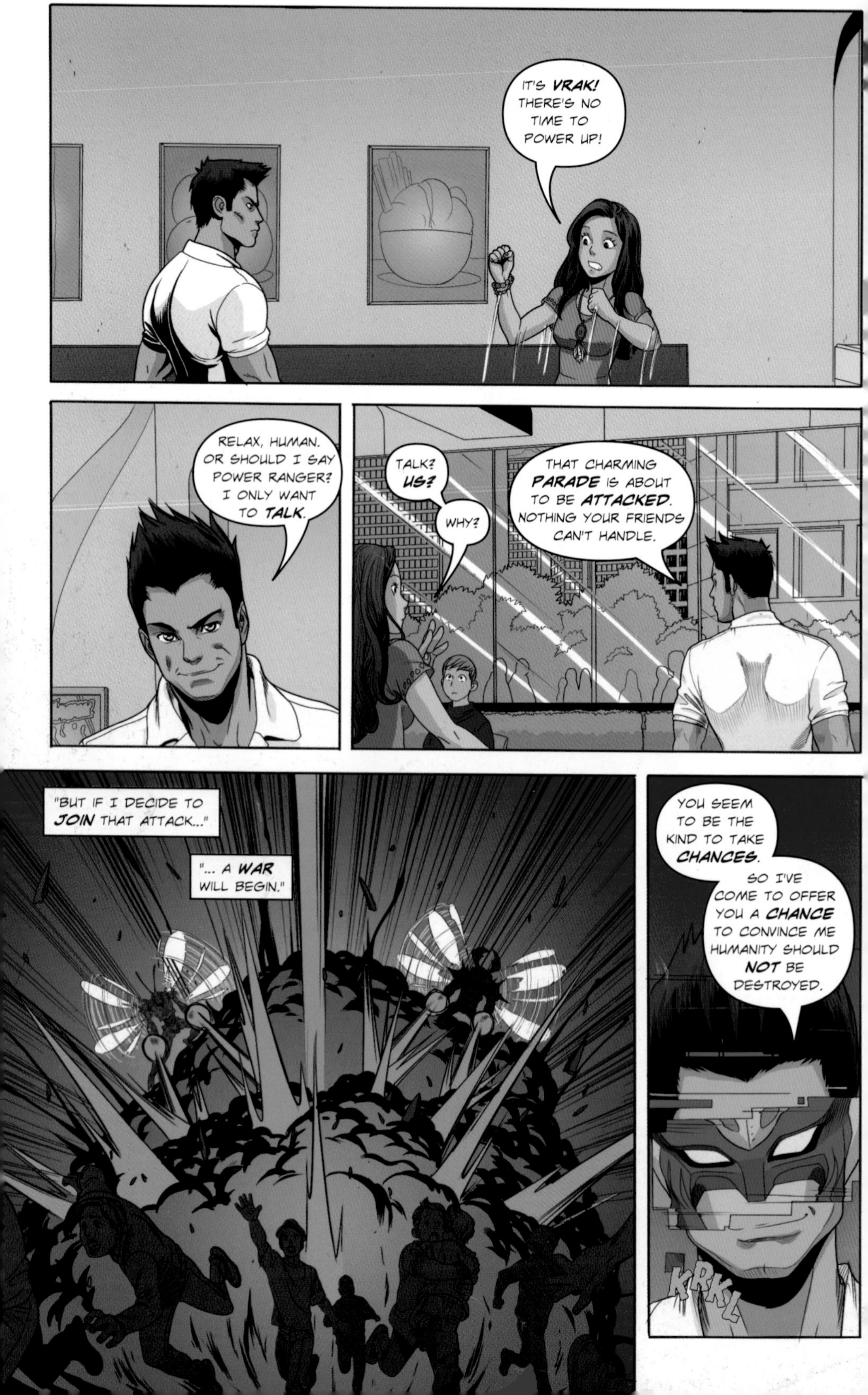
IT'S VRAK! THERE'S NO TIME TO POWER UP!
RELAX, HUMAN. OR SHOULD I SAY POWER RANGER? I ONLY WANT TO TALK.
TALK? US?
WHY?
THAT CHARMING PARADE IS ABOUT TO BE ATTACKED. NOTHING YOUR FRIENDS CAN'T HANDLE.
"BUT IF I DECIDE TO JOIN THAT ATTACK..."
"... A WAR WILL BEGIN."
YOU SEEM TO BE THE KIND TO TAKE CHANCES.
SO I'VE COME TO OFFER YOU A CHANCE TO CONVINCE ME HUMANITY SHOULD NOT BE DESTROYED.
KRKL

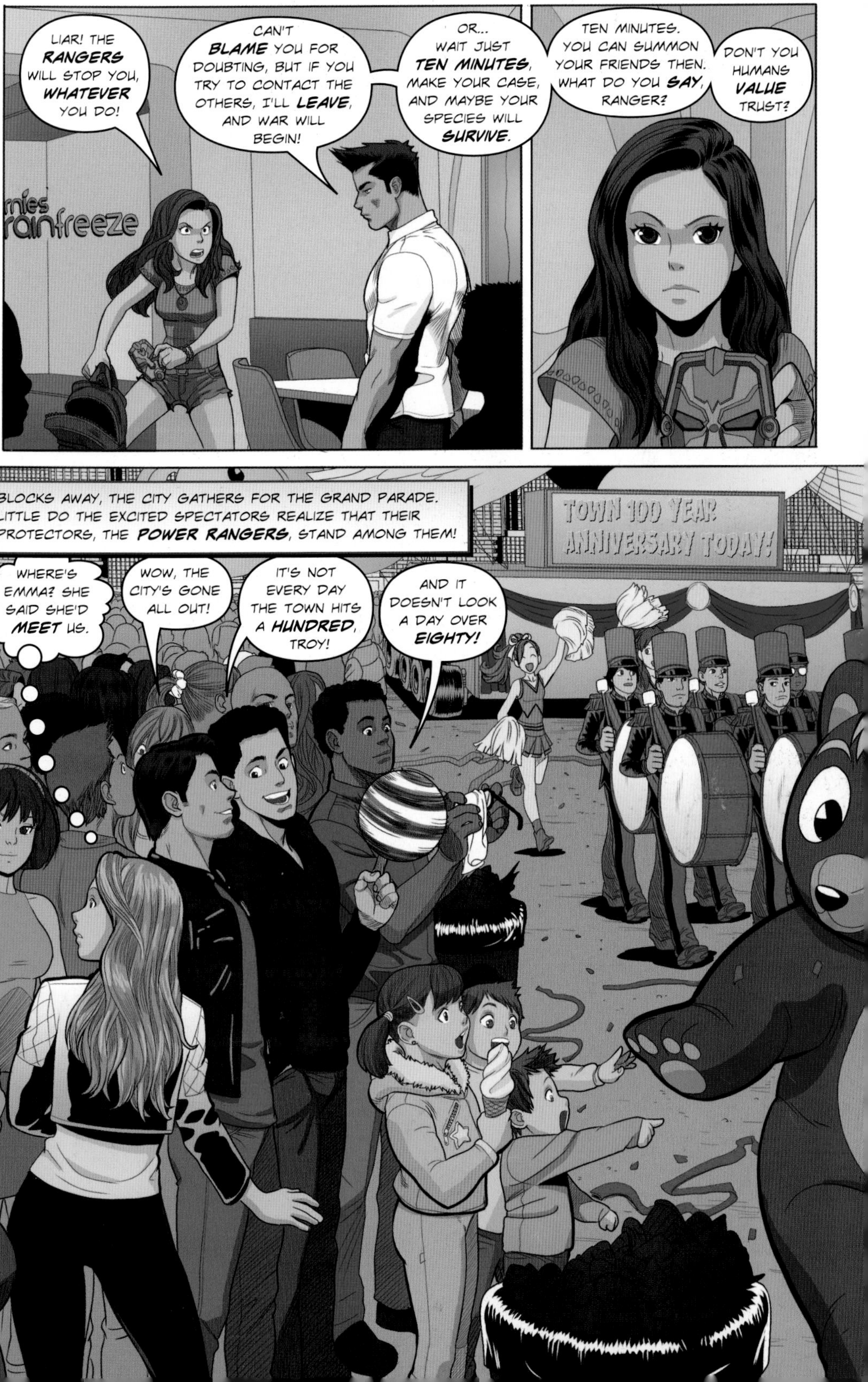
LIAR! THE RANGERS WILL STOP YOU, WHATEVER YOU DO!
CAN'T BLAME YOU FOR DOUBTING, BUT IF YOU TRY TO CONTACT THE OTHERS, I'LL LEAVE, AND WAR WILL BEGIN!
OR... WAIT JUST TEN MINUTES, MAKE YOUR CASE, AND MAYBE YOUR SPECIES WILL SURVIVE.
TEN MINUTES. YOU CAN SUMMON YOUR FRIENDS THEN. WHAT DO YOU SAY, RANGER?
DON'T YOU HUMANS VALUE TRUST?
BLOCKS AWAY, THE CITY GATHERS FOR THE GRAND PARADE. LITTLE DO THE EXCITED SPECTATORS REALIZE THAT THEIR PROTECTORS, THE POWER RANGERS, STAND AMONG THEM!
TOWN 100 YEAR ANNIVERSARY TODAY!
WHERE'S EMMA? SHE SAID SHE'D MEET US.
WOW, THE CITY'S GONE ALL OUT!
IT'S NOT EVERY DAY THE TOWN HITS A HUNDRED, TROY!
AND IT DOESN'T LOOK A DAY OVER EIGHTY!

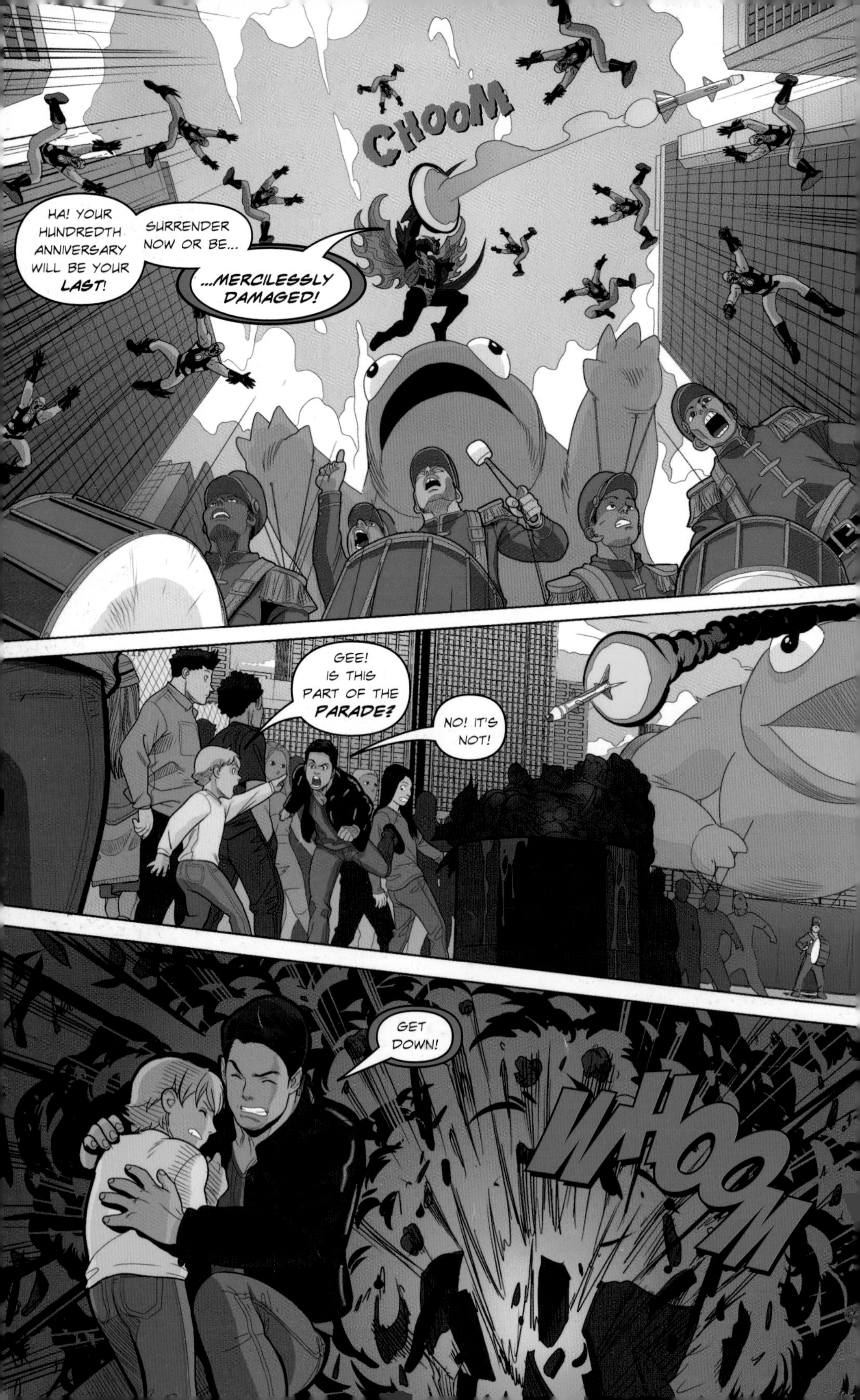
CHOOM
HA! YOUR HUNDREDTH ANNIVERSARY WILL BE YOUR LAST!
SURRENDER NOW OR BE...
...MERCILESSLY DAMAGED!
GEE! IS THIS PART OF THE PARADE?
NO! IT'S NOT!
GET DOWN!
WHOOM

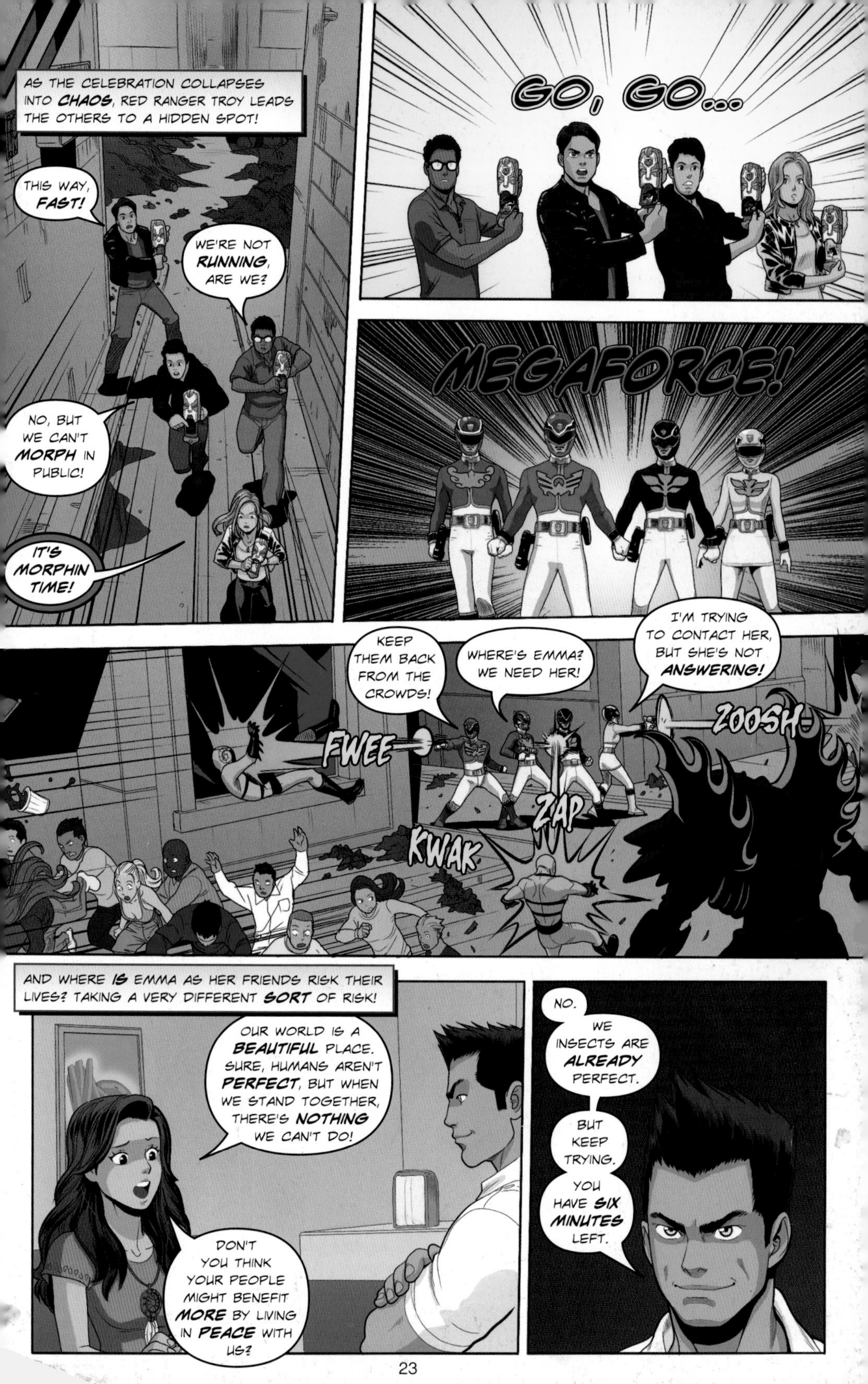
AS THE CELEBRATION COLLAPSES INTO CHAOS, RED RANGER TROY LEADS THE OTHERS TO A HIDDEN SPOT!
THIS WAY, FAST!
WE'RE NOT RUNNING, ARE WE?
NO, BUT WE CAN'T MORPH IN PUBLIC!
IT'S MORPHIN TIME!
GO, GO...
MEGAFORCE!
KEEP THEM BACK FROM THE CROWDS!
WHERE'S EMMA? WE NEED HER!
I'M TRYING TO CONTACT HER, BUT SHE'S NOT ANSWERING!
FWEE
ZOOSH
ZAP
KWAK
AND WHERE IS EMMA AS HER FRIENDS RISK THEIR LIVES? TAKING A VERY DIFFERENT SORT OF RISK!
OUR WORLD IS A BEAUTIFUL PLACE. SURE, HUMANS AREN'T PERFECT, BUT WHEN WE STAND TOGETHER, THERE'S NOTHING WE CAN'T DO!
DON'T YOU THINK YOUR PEOPLE MIGHT BENEFIT MORE BY LIVING IN PEACE WITH US?
NO.
WE INSECTS ARE ALREADY PERFECT.
BUT KEEP TRYING.
YOU HAVE SIX MINUTES LEFT.

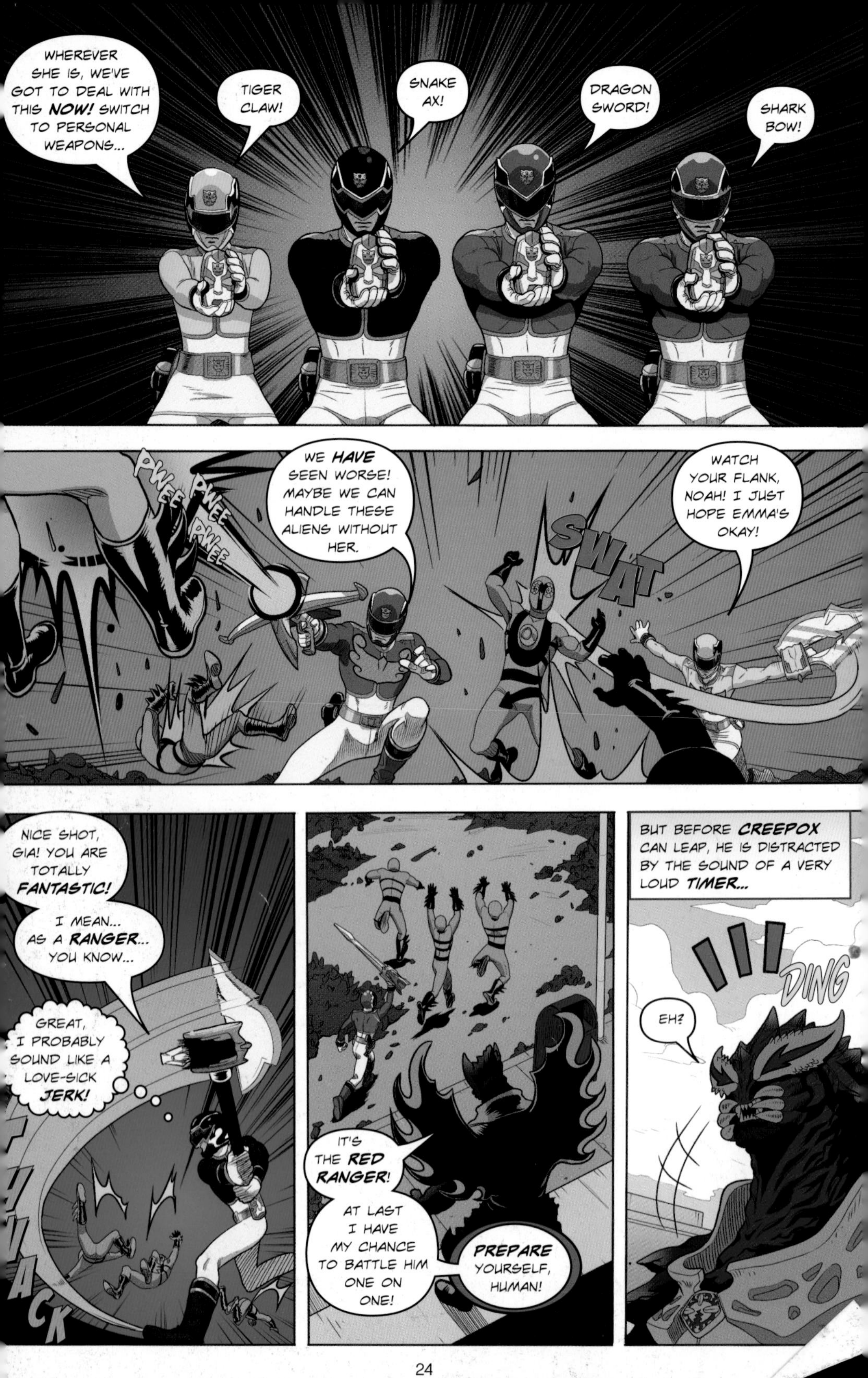
WHEREVER SHE IS, WE'VE GOT TO DEAL WITH THIS NOW! SWITCH TO PERSONAL WEAPONS...
TIGER CLAW!
SNAKE AX!
DRAGON SWORD!
SHARK BOW!
PWEE PWEE PWEE PWEE
WE HAVE SEEN WORSE! MAYBE WE CAN HANDLE THESE ALIENS WITHOUT HER.
SWAT
WATCH YOUR FLANK, NOAH! I JUST HOPE EMMA'S OKAY!
NICE SHOT, GIA! YOU ARE TOTALLY FANTASTIC!
I MEAN... AS A RANGER... YOU KNOW...
GREAT, I PROBABLY SOUND LIKE A LOVE-SICK JERK!
IT'S THE RED RANGER!
AT LAST I HAVE MY CHANCE TO BATTLE HIM ONE ON ONE!
PREPARE YOURSELF, HUMAN!
BUT BEFORE CREEPOX CAN LEAP, HE IS DISTRACTED BY THE SOUND OF A VERY LOUD TIMER...
DING
EH?

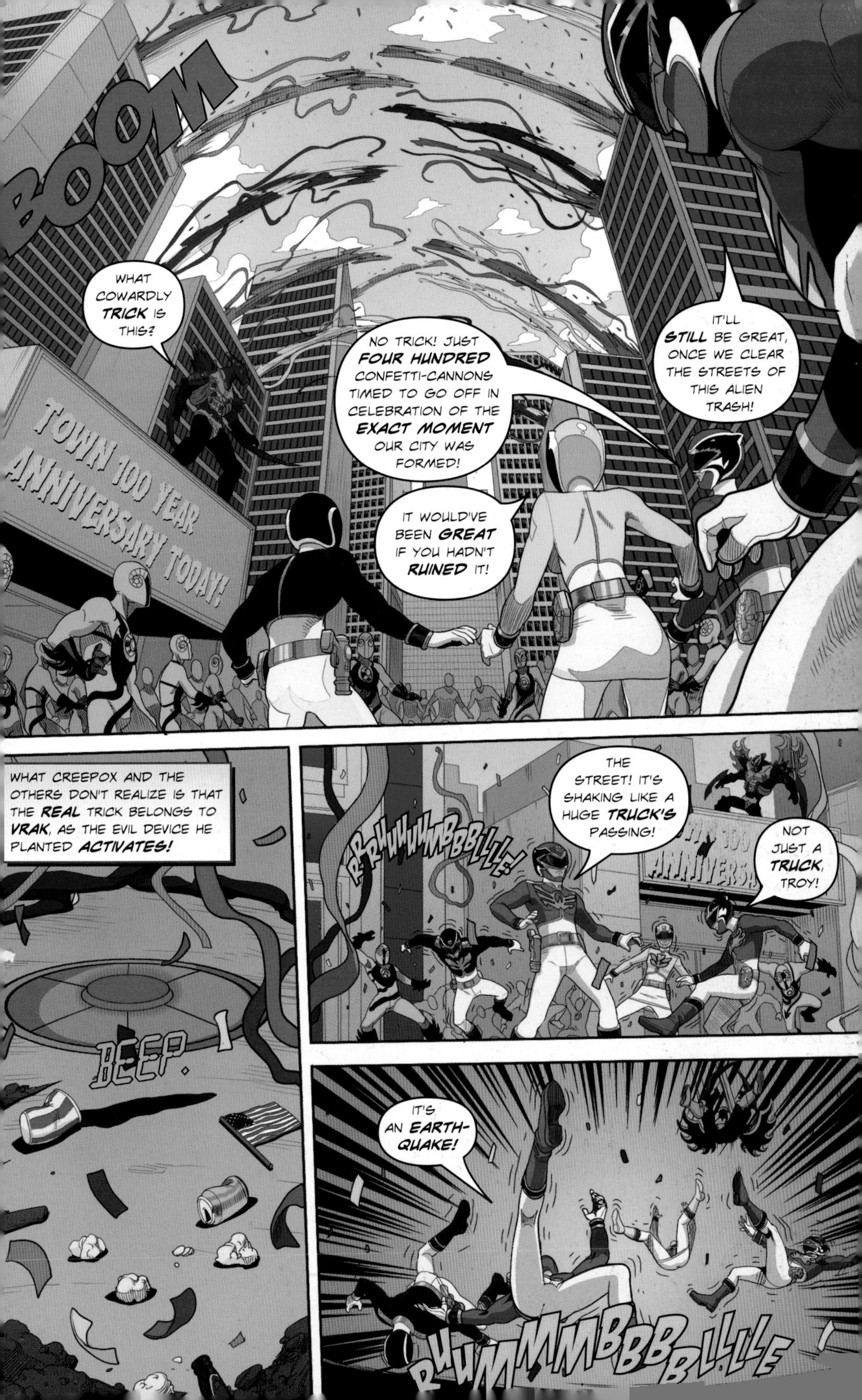
BOOM
WHAT COWARDLY TRICK IS THIS?
NO TRICK! JUST FOUR HUNDRED CONFETTI-CANNONS TIMED TO GO OFF IN CELEBRATION OF THE EXACT MOMENT OUR CITY WAS FORMED!
IT'LL STILL BE GREAT, ONCE WE CLEAR THE STREETS OF THIS ALIEN TRASH!
IT WOULD'VE BEEN GREAT IF YOU HADN'T RUINED IT!
TOWN 100 YEAR ANNIVERSARY TODAY!
WHAT CREEPOX AND THE OTHERS DON'T REALIZE IS THAT THE REAL TRICK BELONGS TO VRAK, AS THE EVIL DEVICE HE PLANTED ACTIVATES!
BEEP.
RRRUUUUMMBBBLLLE!
THE STREET! IT'S SHAKING LIKE A HUGE TRUCK'S PASSING!
NOT JUST A TRUCK, TROY!
IT'S AN EARTH-QUAKE!
RUUMMMMBBBBLLLE

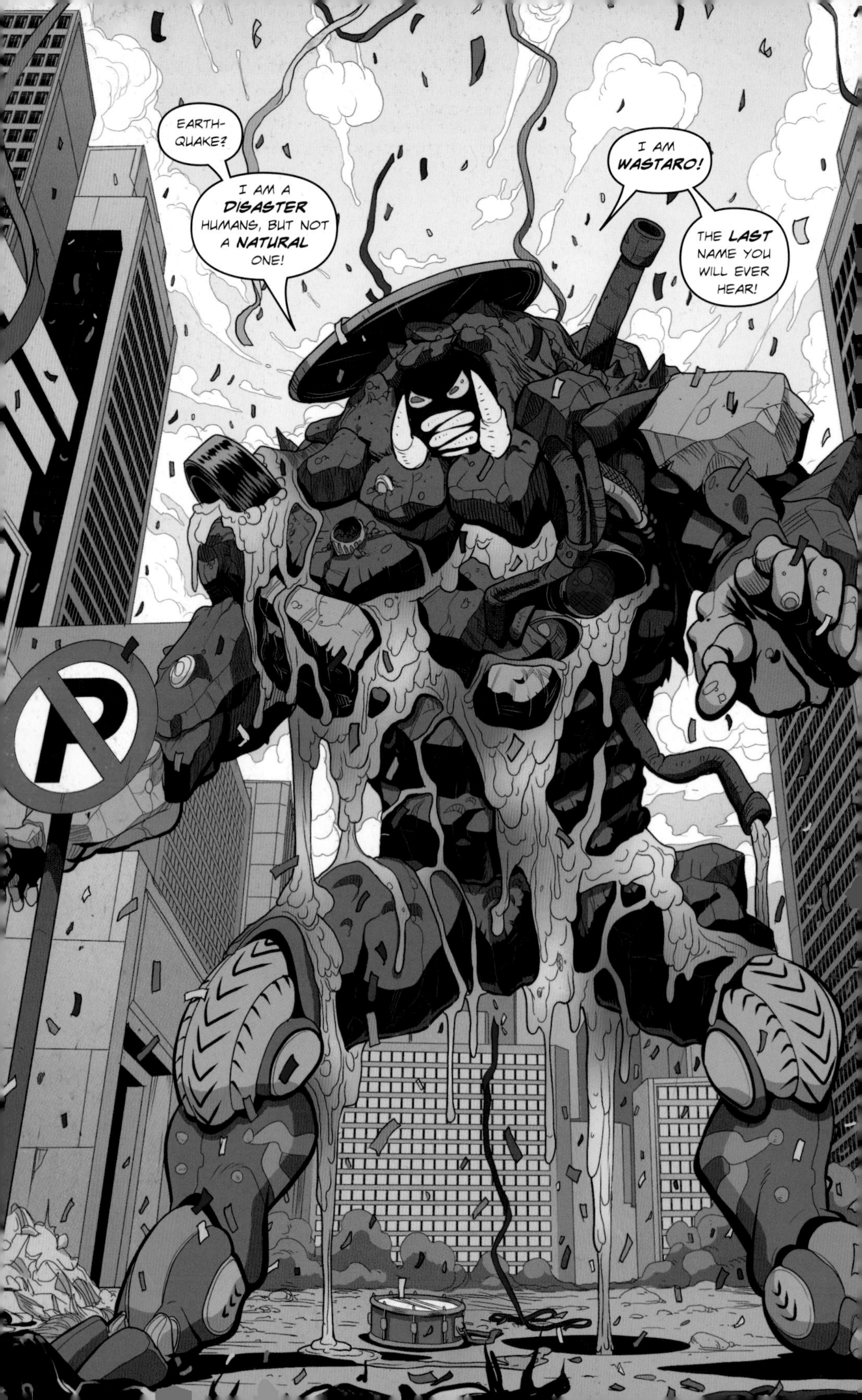
EARTH-QUAKE?
I AM A DISASTER HUMANS, BUT NOT A NATURAL ONE!
I AM WASTARO!
THE LAST NAME YOU WILL EVER HEAR!

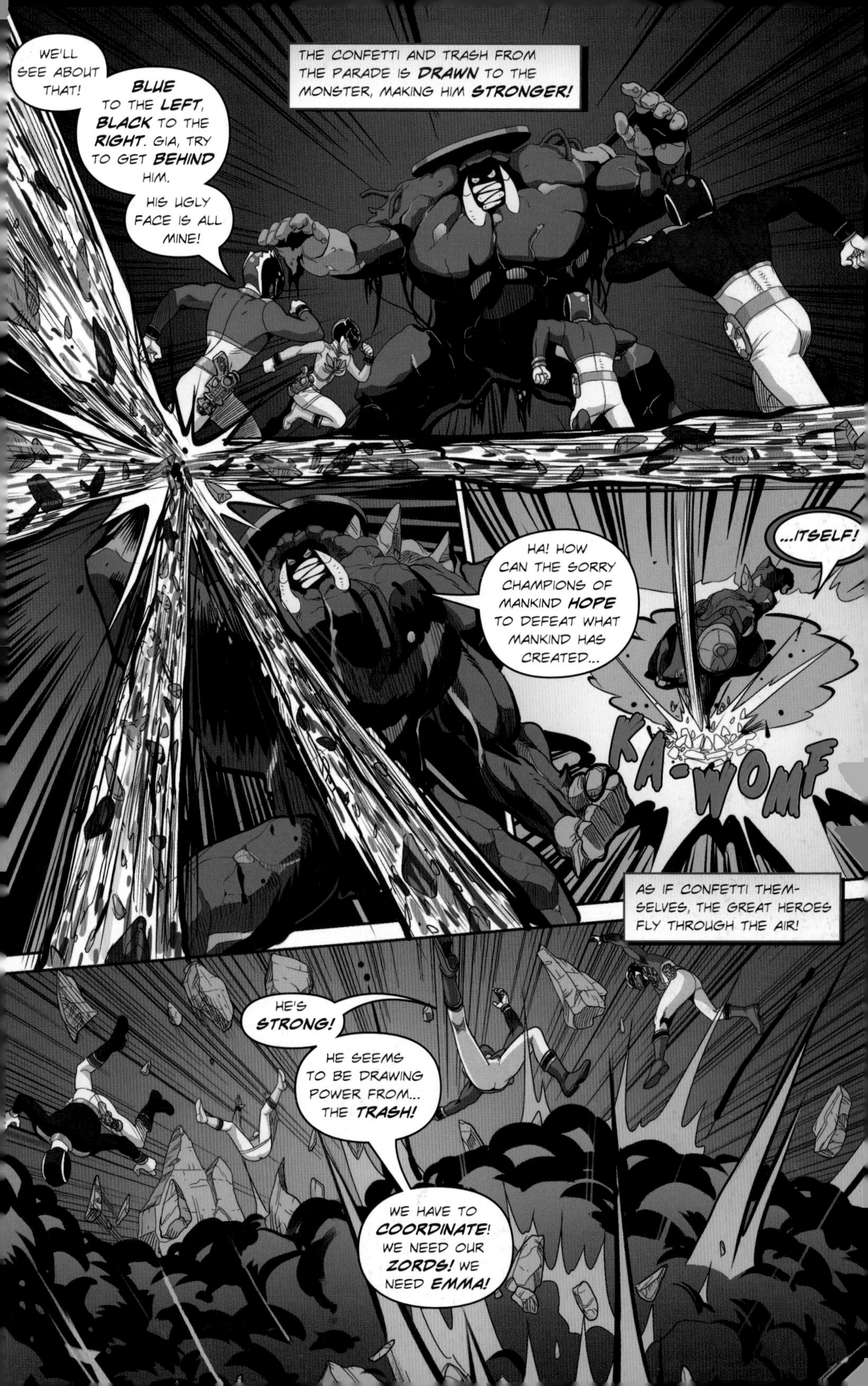
THE CONFETTI AND TRASH FROM THE PARADE IS DRAWN TO THE MONSTER, MAKING HIM STRONGER!
WE'LL SEE ABOUT THAT!
BLUE TO THE LEFT, BLACK TO THE RIGHT. GIA, TRY TO GET BEHIND HIM.
HIS UGLY FACE IS ALL MINE!
HA! HOW CAN THE SORRY CHAMPIONS OF MANKIND HOPE TO DEFEAT WHAT MANKIND HAS CREATED...
...ITSELF!
KA-WOMF
AS IF CONFETTI THEMSELVES, THE GREAT HEROES FLY THROUGH THE AIR!
HE'S STRONG!
HE SEEMS TO BE DRAWING POWER FROM... THE TRASH!
WE HAVE TO COORDINATE! WE NEED OUR ZORDS! WE NEED EMMA!

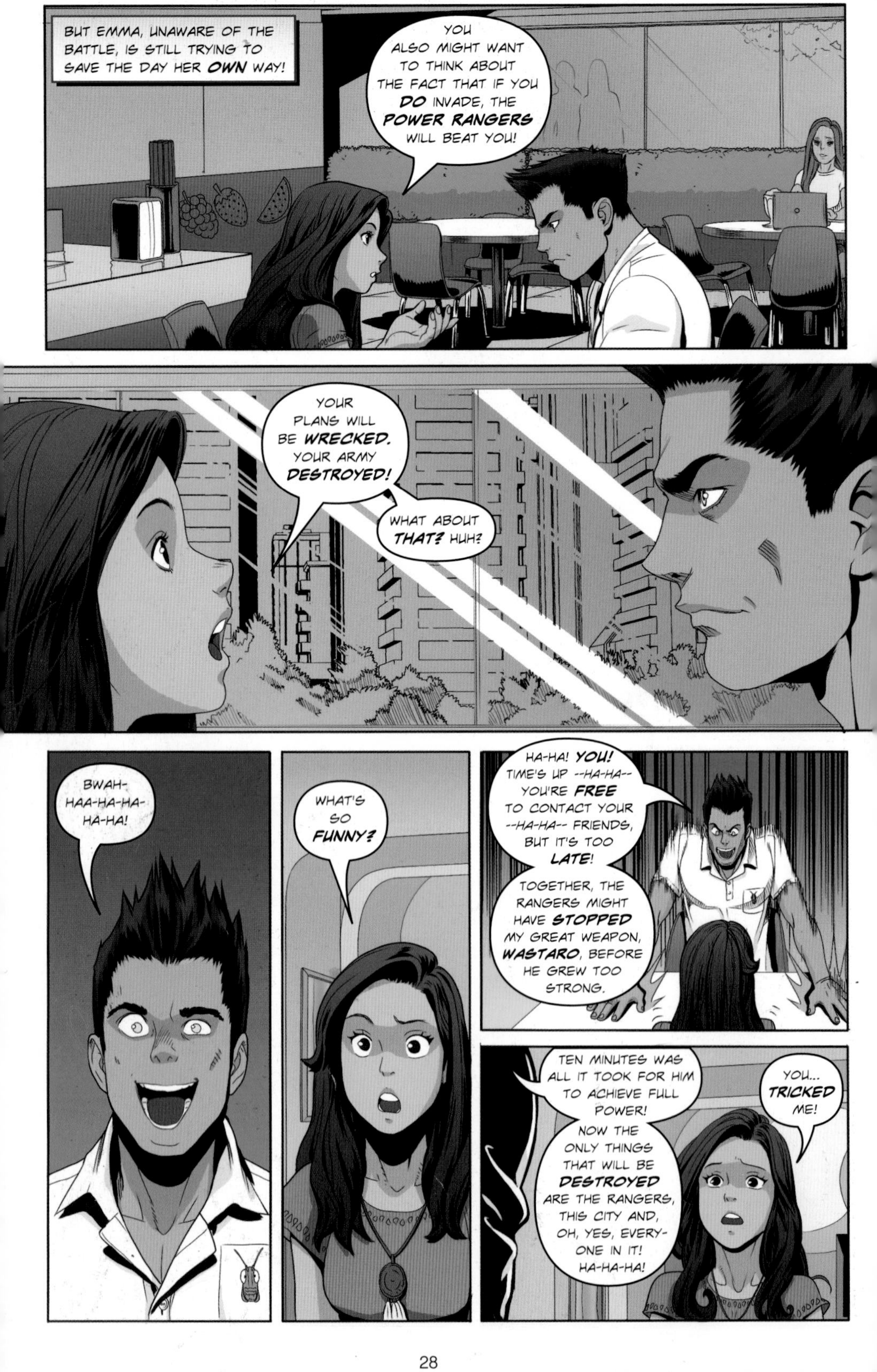
BUT EMMA, UNAWARE OF THE BATTLE, IS STILL TRYING TO SAVE THE DAY HER OWN WAY!
YOU ALSO MIGHT WANT TO THINK ABOUT THE FACT THAT IF YOU DO INVADE, THE POWER RANGERS WILL BEAT YOU!
YOUR PLANS WILL BE WRECKED. YOUR ARMY DESTROYED!
WHAT ABOUT THAT? HUH?
BWAH-HAA-HA-HA-HA-HA!
WHAT'S SO FUNNY?
HA-HA! YOU! TIME'S UP --HA-HA-- YOU'RE FREE TO CONTACT YOUR --HA-HA-- FRIENDS, BUT IT'S TOO LATE!
TOGETHER, THE RANGERS MIGHT HAVE STOPPED MY GREAT WEAPON, WASTARO, BEFORE HE GREW TOO STRONG.
TEN MINUTES WAS ALL IT TOOK FOR HIM TO ACHIEVE FULL POWER!
NOW THE ONLY THINGS THAT WILL BE DESTROYED ARE THE RANGERS, THIS CITY AND, OH, YES, EVERY-ONE IN IT! HA-HA-HA!
YOU... TRICKED ME!

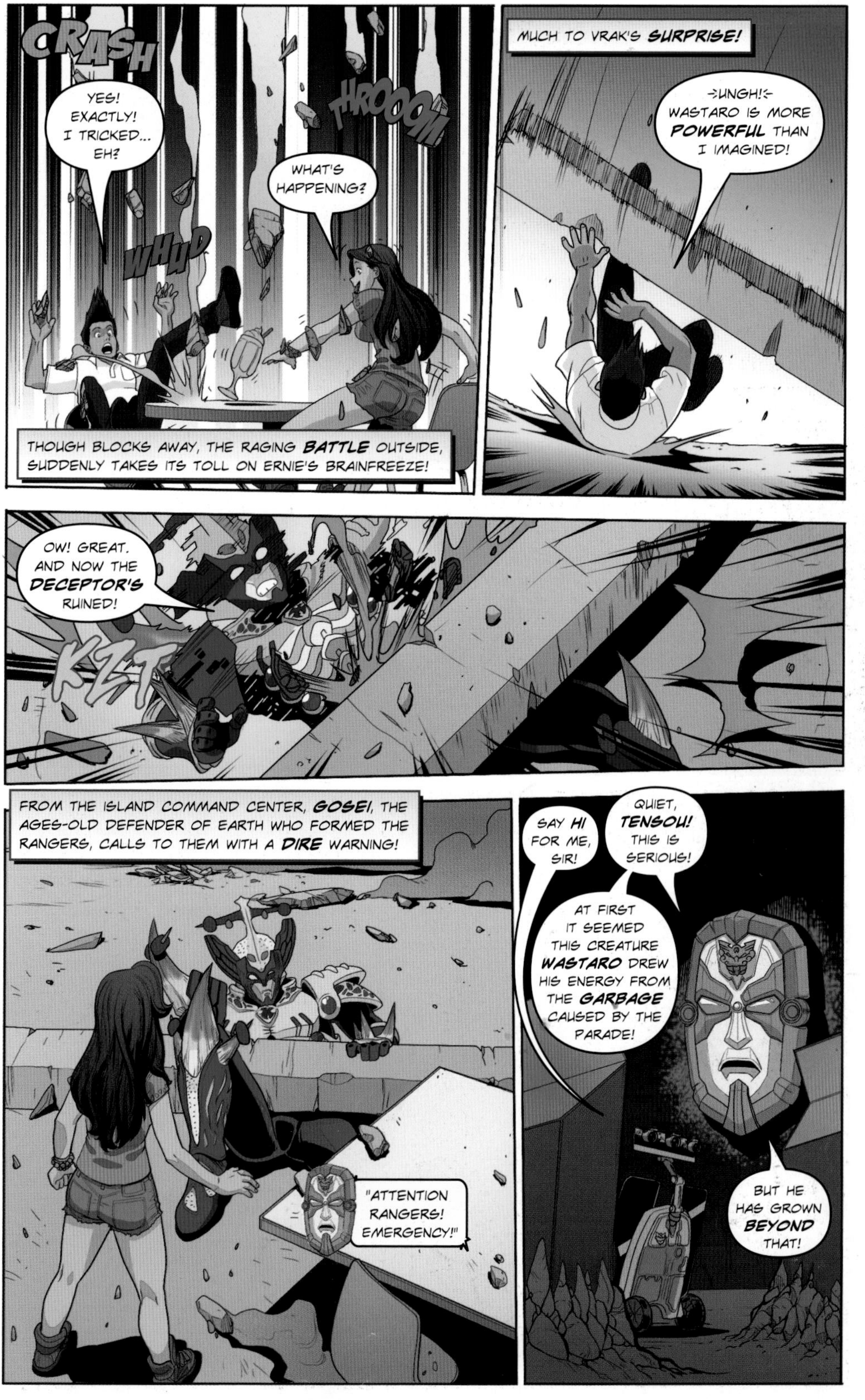
CRASH
YES! EXACTLY! I TRICKED... EH?
THROOOM
WHAT'S HAPPENING?
WHUD
THOUGH BLOCKS AWAY, THE RAGING BATTLE OUTSIDE, SUDDENLY TAKES ITS TOLL ON ERNIE'S BRAINFREEZE!
MUCH TO VRAK'S SURPRISE!
UNGH! WASTARO IS MORE POWERFUL THAN I IMAGINED!
OW! GREAT. AND NOW THE DECEPTOR'S RUINED!
KZZT
FROM THE ISLAND COMMAND CENTER, GOSEI, THE AGES-OLD DEFENDER OF EARTH WHO FORMED THE RANGERS, CALLS TO THEM WITH A DIRE WARNING!
"ATTENTION RANGERS! EMERGENCY!"
SAY HI FOR ME, SIR!
QUIET, TENSOU! THIS IS SERIOUS!
AT FIRST IT SEEMED THIS CREATURE WASTARO DREW HIS ENERGY FROM THE GARBAGE CAUSED BY THE PARADE!
BUT HE HAS GROWN BEYOND THAT!

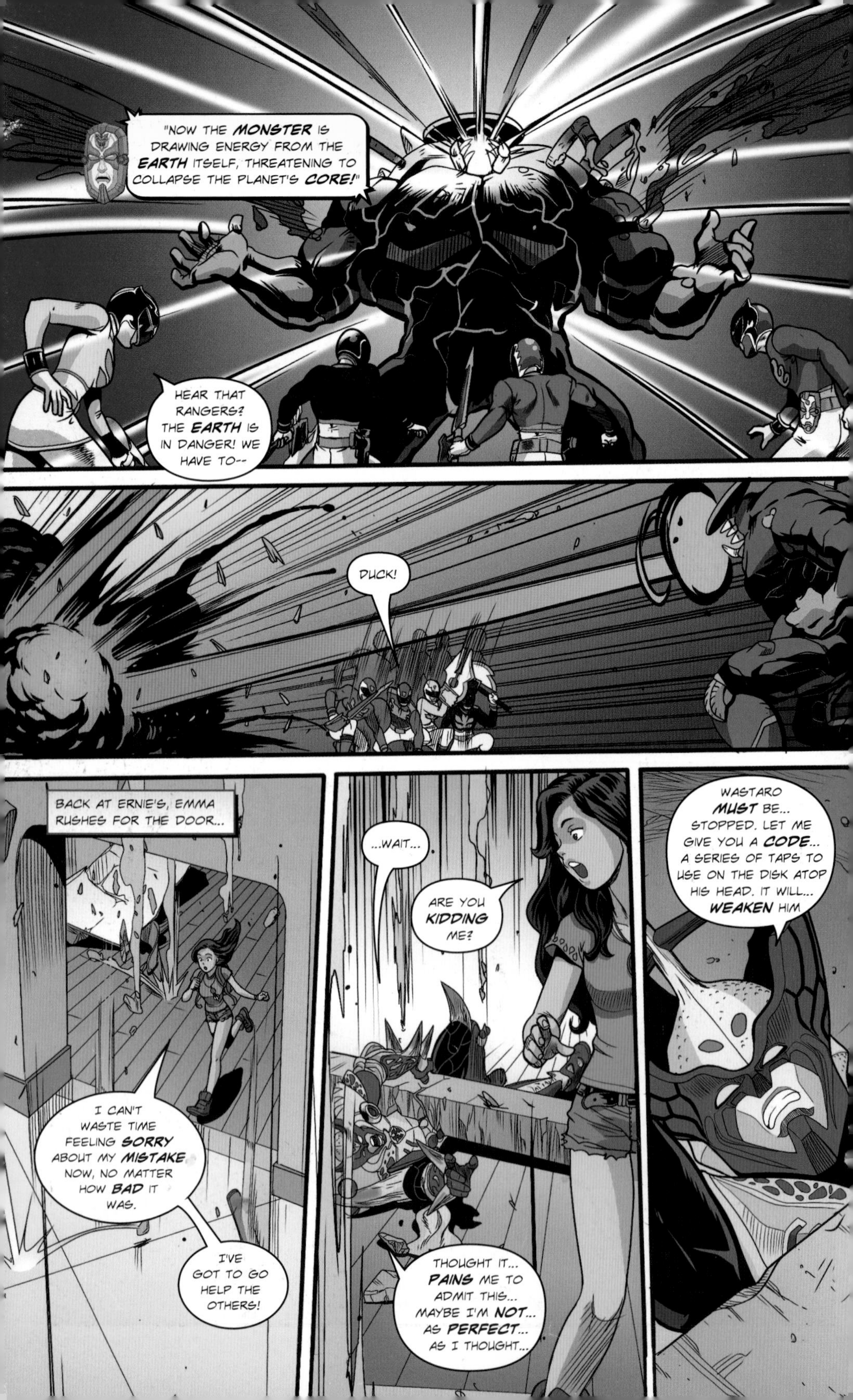
"NOW THE MONSTER IS DRAWING ENERGY FROM THE EARTH ITSELF, THREATENING TO COLLAPSE THE PLANET'S CORE!"
HEAR THAT RANGERS? THE EARTH IS IN DANGER! WE HAVE TO--
DUCK!
BACK AT ERNIE'S, EMMA RUSHES FOR THE DOOR...
I CAN'T WASTE TIME FEELING SORRY ABOUT MY MISTAKE NOW, NO MATTER HOW BAD IT WAS.
I'VE GOT TO GO HELP THE OTHERS!
...WAIT...
ARE YOU KIDDING ME?
THOUGHT IT... PAINS ME TO ADMIT THIS... MAYBE I'M NOT... AS PERFECT... AS I THOUGHT...
WASTARO MUST BE... STOPPED. LET ME GIVE YOU A CODE... A SERIES OF TAPS TO USE ON THE DISK ATOP HIS HEAD. IT WILL... WEAKEN HIM

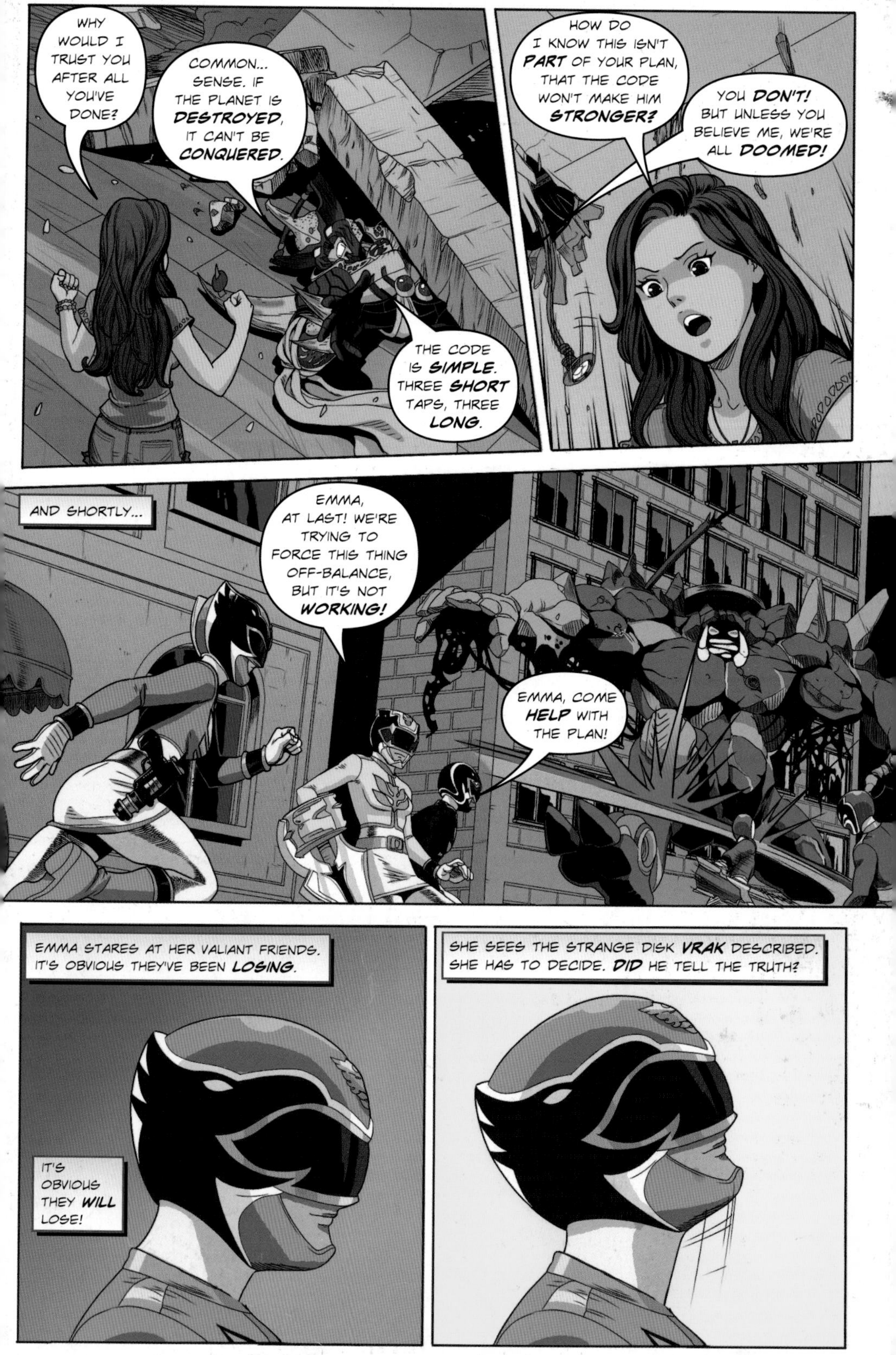
WHY WOULD I TRUST YOU AFTER ALL YOU'VE DONE?
COMMON... SENSE. IF THE PLANET IS DESTROYED, IT CAN'T BE CONQUERED.
THE CODE IS SIMPLE. THREE SHORT TAPS, THREE LONG.
HOW DO I KNOW THIS ISN'T PART OF YOUR PLAN, THAT THE CODE WON'T MAKE HIM STRONGER?
YOU DON'T! BUT UNLESS YOU BELIEVE ME, WE'RE ALL DOOMED!
AND SHORTLY...
EMMA, AT LAST! WE'RE TRYING TO FORCE THIS THING OFF-BALANCE, BUT IT'S NOT WORKING!
EMMA, COME HELP WITH THE PLAN!
EMMA STARES AT HER VALIANT FRIENDS. IT'S OBVIOUS THEY'VE BEEN LOSING.
IT'S OBVIOUS THEY WILL LOSE!
SHE SEES THE STRANGE DISK VRAK DESCRIBED. SHE HAS TO DECIDE. DID HE TELL THE TRUTH?

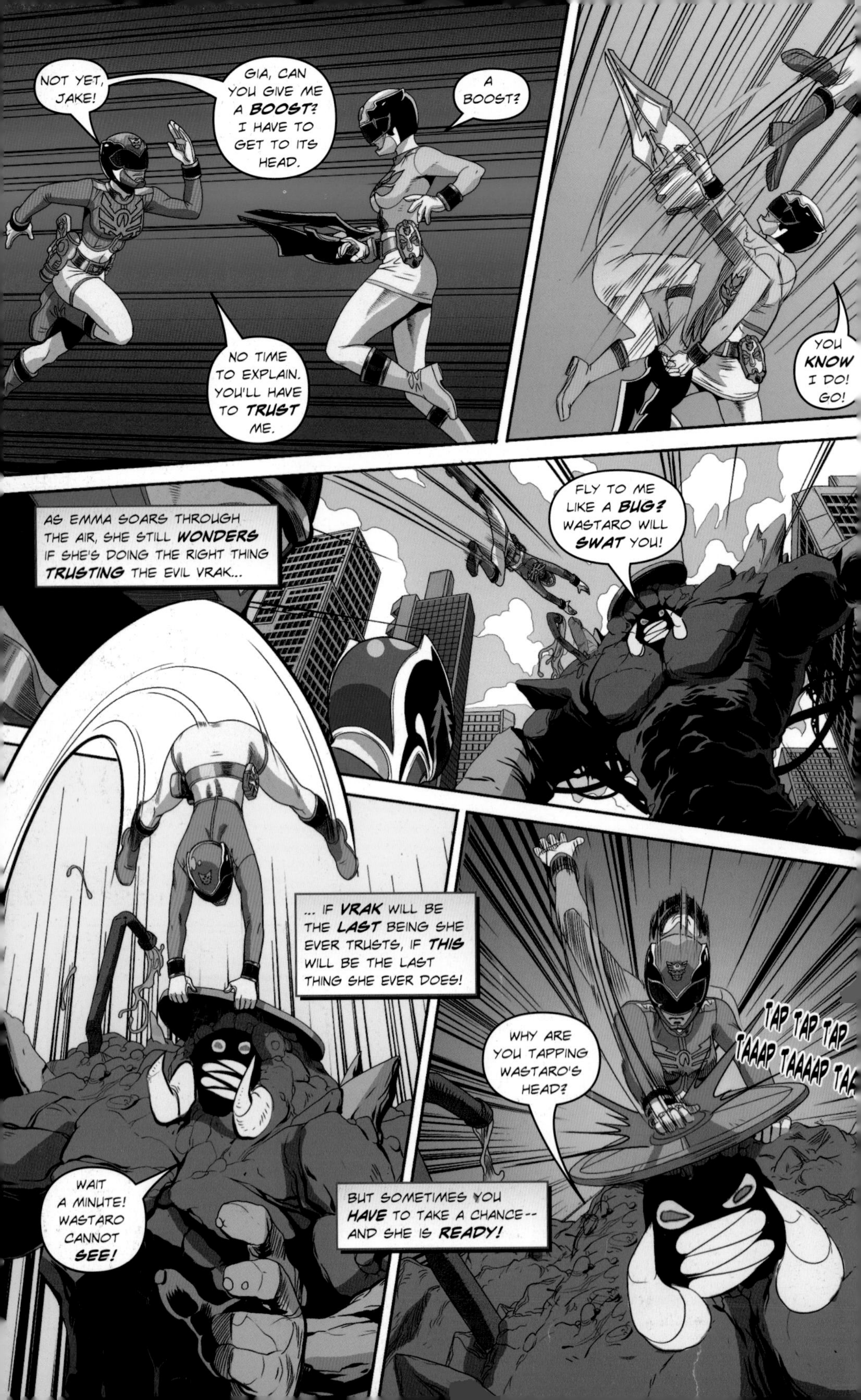
NOT YET, JAKE!
GIA, CAN YOU GIVE ME A BOOST? I HAVE TO GET TO ITS HEAD.
A BOOST?
NO TIME TO EXPLAIN. YOU'LL HAVE TO TRUST ME.
YOU KNOW I DO! GO!
AS EMMA SOARS THROUGH THE AIR, SHE STILL WONDERS IF SHE'S DOING THE RIGHT THING TRUSTING THE EVIL VRAK...
FLY TO ME LIKE A BUG? WASTARO WILL SWAT YOU!
... IF VRAK WILL BE THE LAST BEING SHE EVER TRUSTS, IF THIS WILL BE THE LAST THING SHE EVER DOES!
WAIT A MINUTE! WASTARO CANNOT SEE!
WHY ARE YOU TAPPING WASTARO'S HEAD?
TAP TAP TAP TAAAP TAAAAP
BUT SOMETIMES YOU HAVE TO TAKE A CHANCE-- AND SHE IS READY!

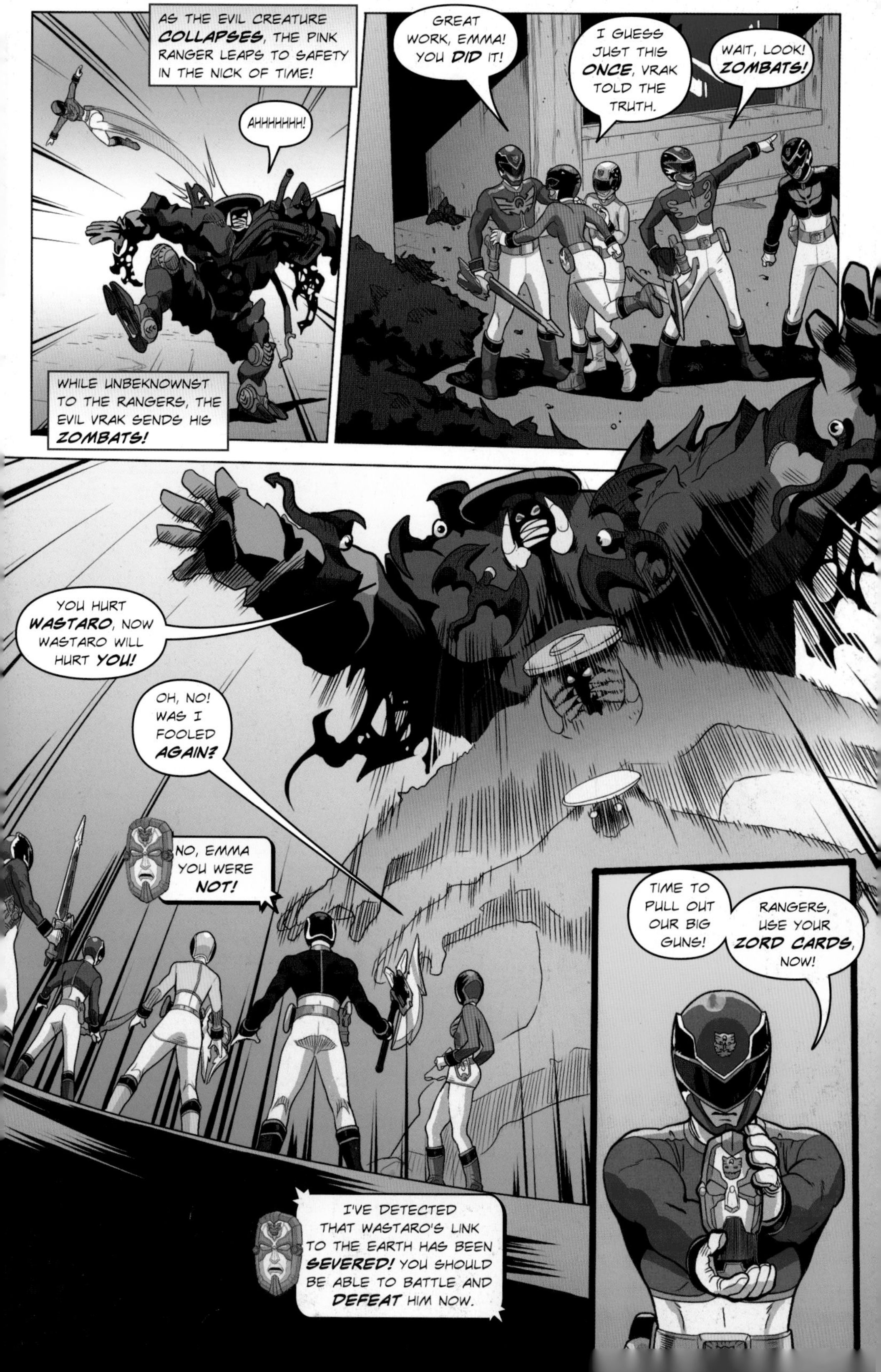
AS THE EVIL CREATURE COLLAPSES, THE PINK RANGER LEAPS TO SAFETY IN THE NICK OF TIME!
AHHHHHHH!
WHILE UNBEKNOWNST TO THE RANGERS, THE EVIL VRAK SENDS HIS ZOMBATS!
GREAT WORK, EMMA! YOU DID IT!
I GUESS JUST THIS ONCE, VRAK TOLD THE TRUTH.
WAIT, LOOK! ZOMBATS!
YOU HURT WASTARO, NOW WASTARO WILL HURT YOU!
OH, NO! WAS I FOOLED AGAIN?
NO, EMMA YOU WERE NOT!
TIME TO PULL OUT OUR BIG GUNS!
RANGERS, USE YOUR ZORD CARDS, NOW!
I'VE DETECTED THAT WASTARO'S LINK TO THE EARTH HAS BEEN SEVERED! YOU SHOULD BE ABLE TO BATTLE AND DEFEAT HIM NOW.

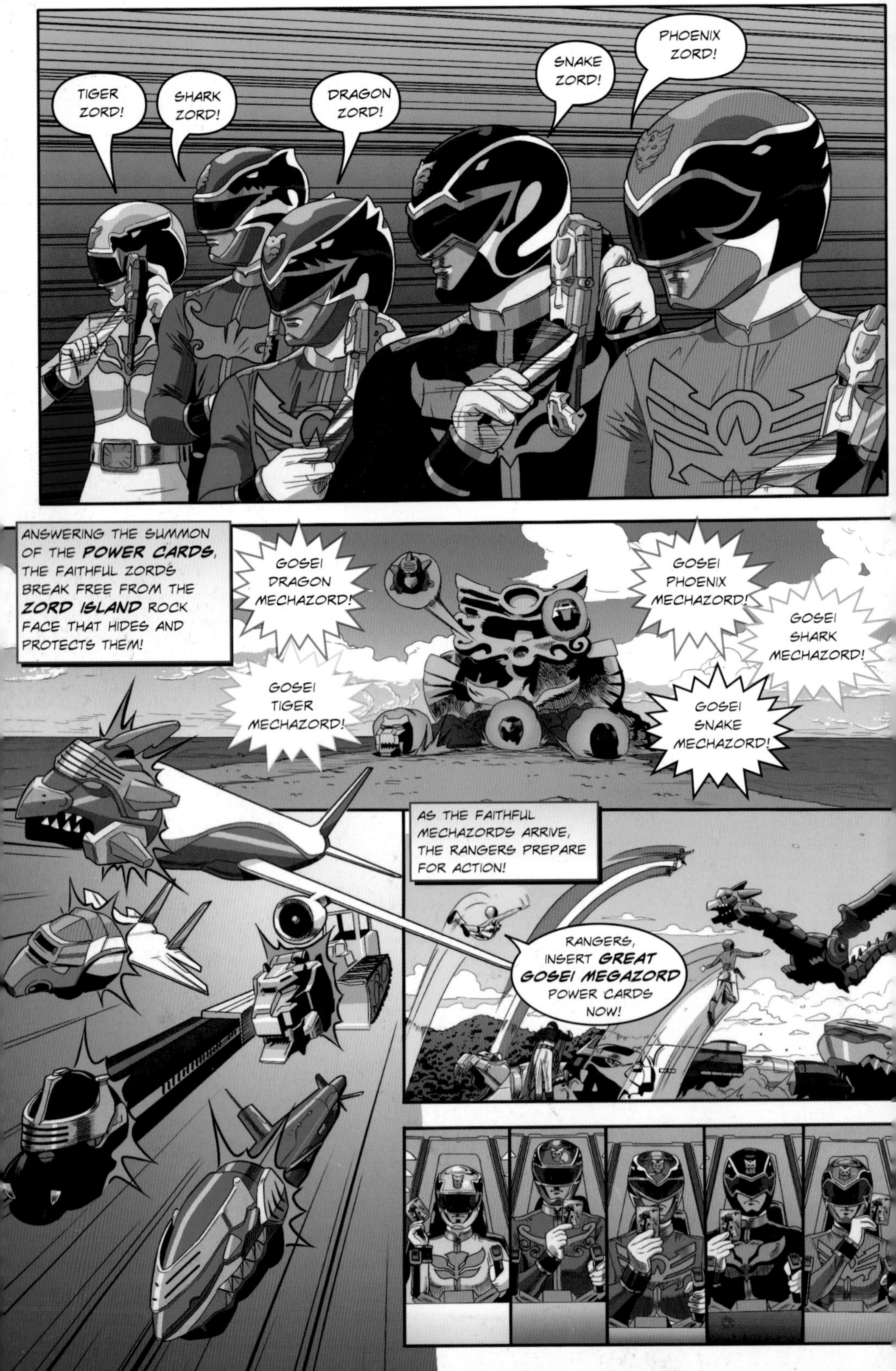
TIGER ZORD!
SHARK ZORD!
DRAGON ZORD!
SNAKE ZORD!
PHOENIX ZORD!
ANSWERING THE SUMMON OF THE **POWER CARDS**, THE FAITHFUL ZORDS BREAK FREE FROM THE **ZORD ISLAND** ROCK FACE THAT HIDES AND PROTECTS THEM!
GOSEI DRAGON MECHAZORD!
GOSEI PHOENIX MECHAZORD!
GOSEI SHARK MECHAZORD!
GOSEI TIGER MECHAZORD!
GOSEI SNAKE MECHAZORD!
AS THE FAITHFUL MECHAZORDS ARRIVE, THE RANGERS PREPARE FOR ACTION!
RANGERS, INSERT **GREAT GOSEI MEGAZORD** POWER CARDS NOW!

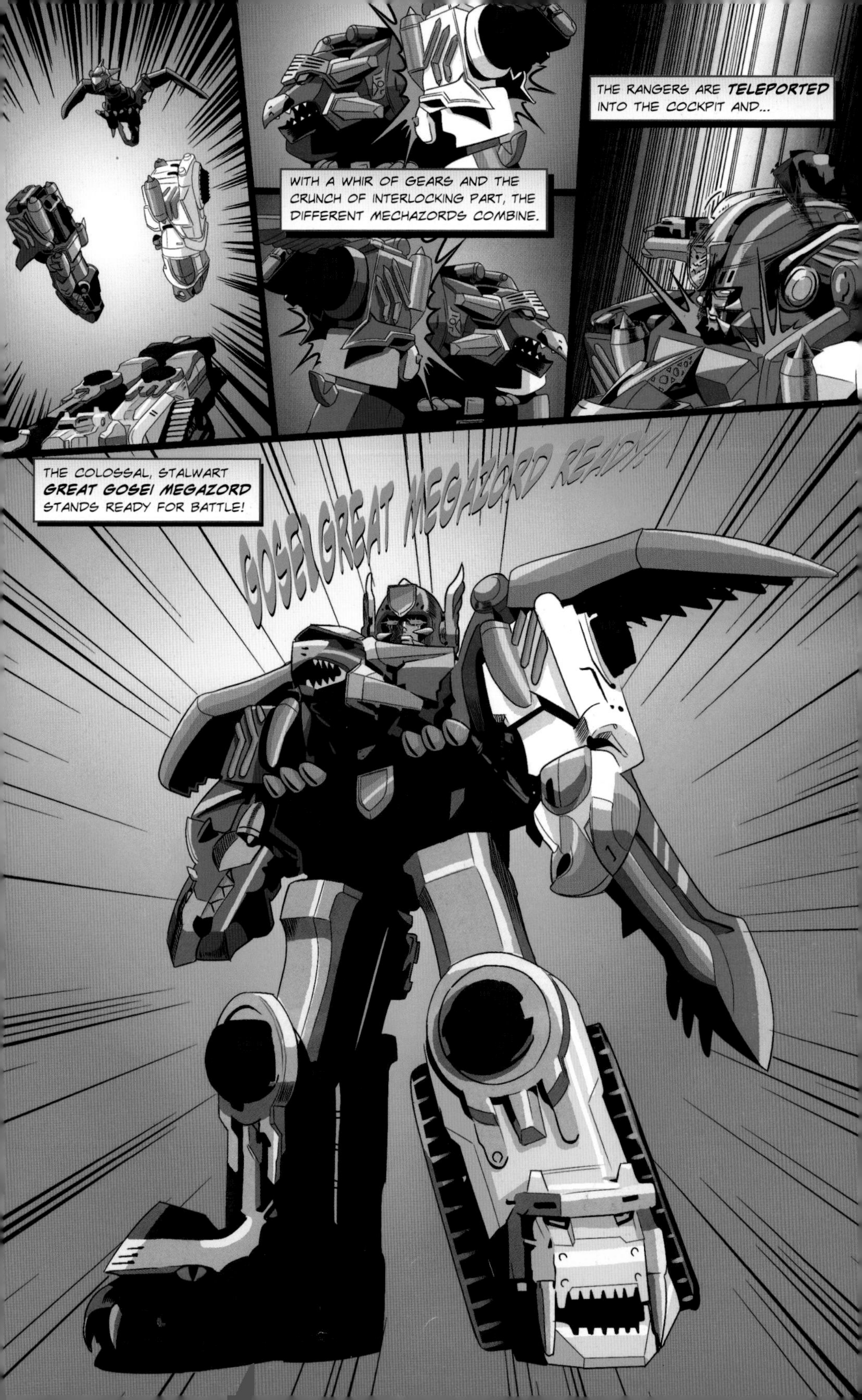

WITH A WHIR OF GEARS AND THE CRUNCH OF INTERLOCKING PART, THE DIFFERENT MECHAZORDS COMBINE.
THE RANGERS ARE TELEPORTED INTO THE COCKPIT AND...
THE COLOSSAL, STALWART GREAT GOSEI MEGAZORD STANDS READY FOR BATTLE!
GOSEI GREAT MEGAZORD READY!

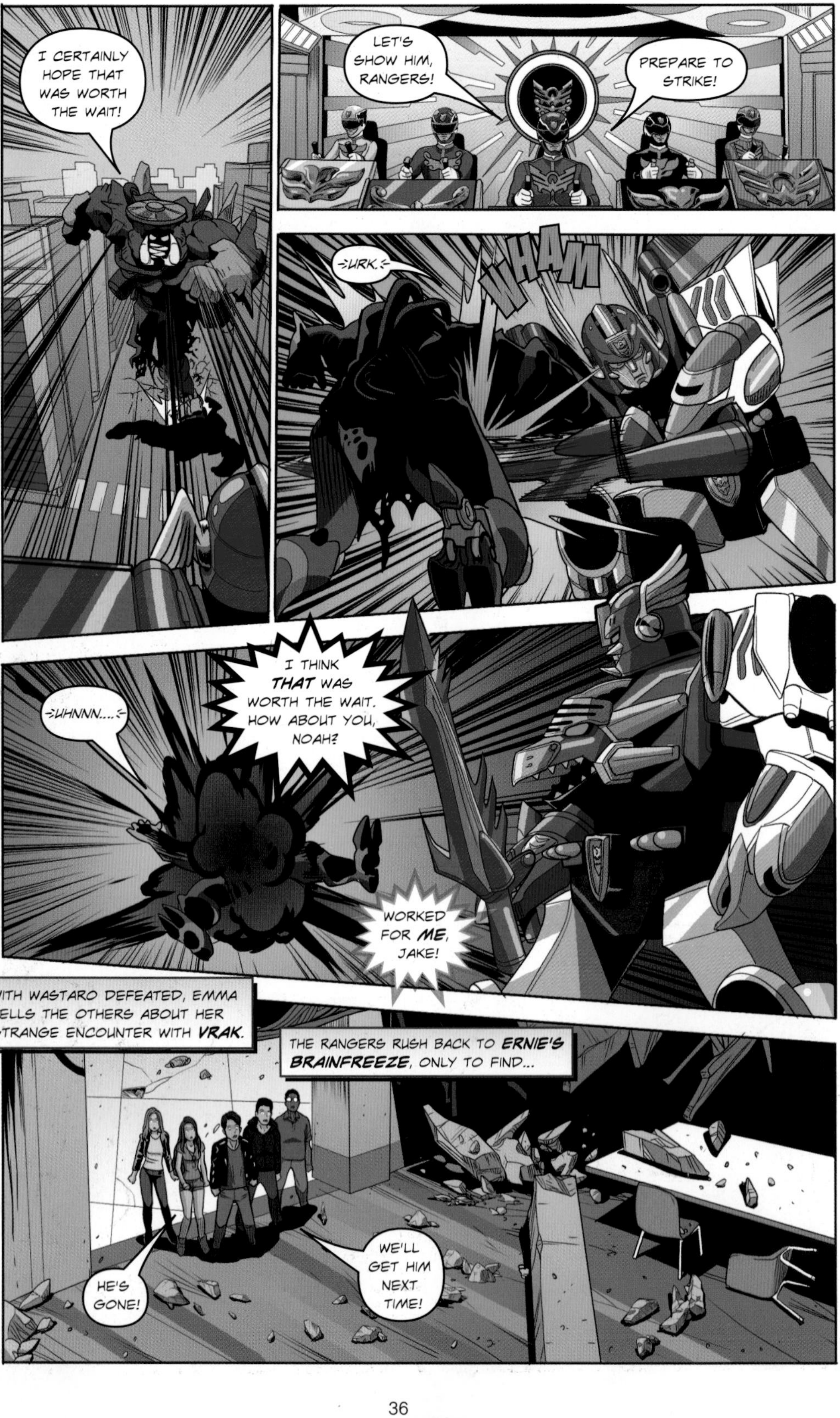
I CERTAINLY HOPE THAT WAS WORTH THE WAIT!
LET'S SHOW HIM, RANGERS!
PREPARE TO STRIKE!
URK.
WHAM
UHNNN....
I THINK THAT WAS WORTH THE WAIT. HOW ABOUT YOU, NOAH?
WORKED FOR ME, JAKE!
WITH WASTARO DEFEATED, EMMA TELLS THE OTHERS ABOUT HER STRANGE ENCOUNTER WITH VRAK.
THE RANGERS RUSH BACK TO ERNIE'S BRAINFREEZE, ONLY TO FIND...
HE'S GONE!
WE'LL GET HIM NEXT TIME!

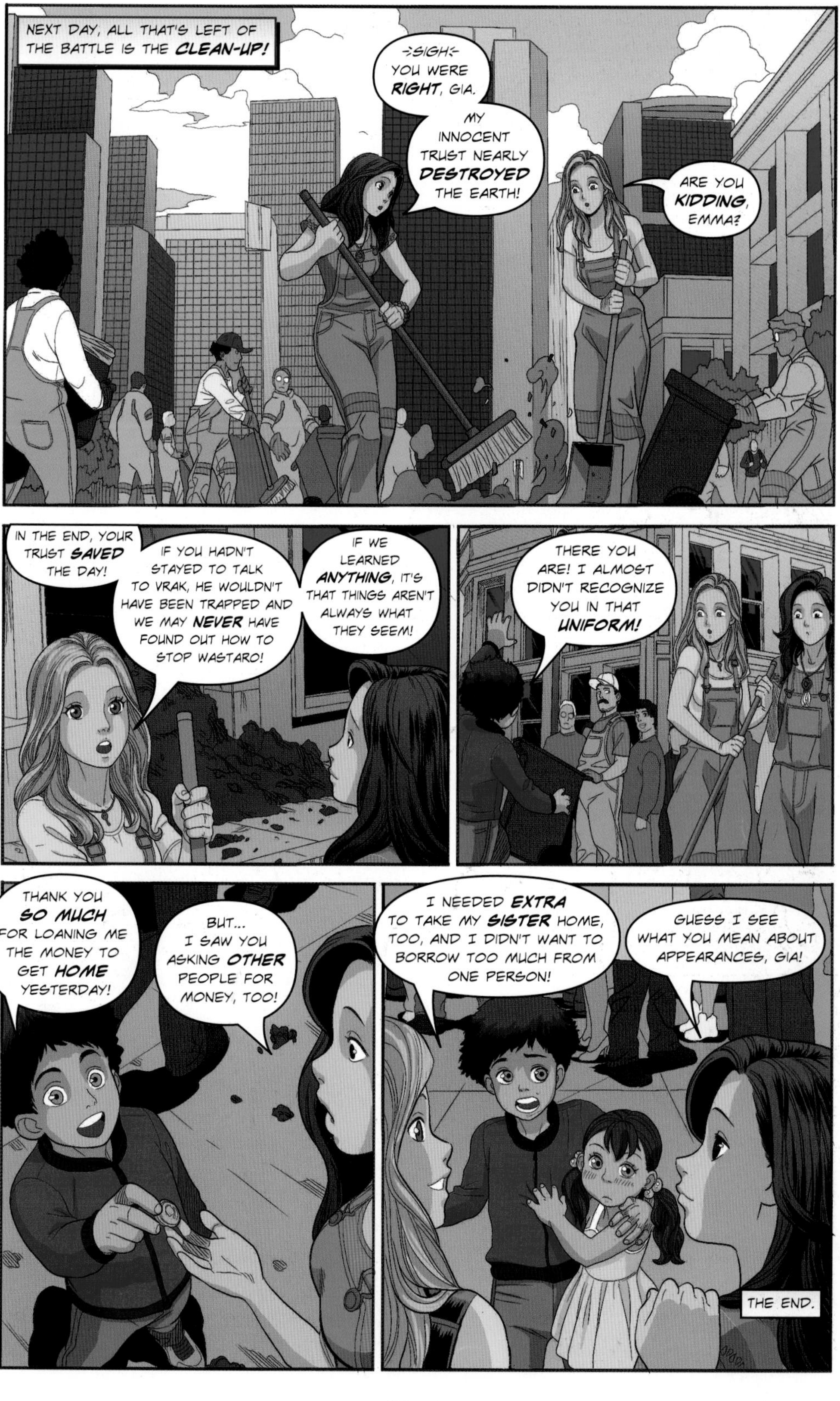
NEXT DAY, ALL THAT'S LEFT OF THE BATTLE IS THE CLEAN-UP!
-SIGH- YOU WERE RIGHT, GIA.
MY INNOCENT TRUST NEARLY DESTROYED THE EARTH!
ARE YOU KIDDING, EMMA?
IN THE END, YOUR TRUST SAVED THE DAY!
IF YOU HADN'T STAYED TO TALK TO VRAK, HE WOULDN'T HAVE BEEN TRAPPED AND WE MAY NEVER HAVE FOUND OUT HOW TO STOP WASTARO!
IF WE LEARNED ANYTHING, IT'S THAT THINGS AREN'T ALWAYS WHAT THEY SEEM!
THERE YOU ARE! I ALMOST DIDN'T RECOGNIZE YOU IN THAT UNIFORM!
THANK YOU SO MUCH FOR LOANING ME THE MONEY TO GET HOME YESTERDAY!
BUT... I SAW YOU ASKING OTHER PEOPLE FOR MONEY, TOO!
I NEEDED EXTRA TO TAKE MY SISTER HOME, TOO, AND I DIDN'T WANT TO BORROW TOO MUCH FROM ONE PERSON!
GUESS I SEE WHAT YOU MEAN ABOUT APPEARANCES, GIA!
THE END.

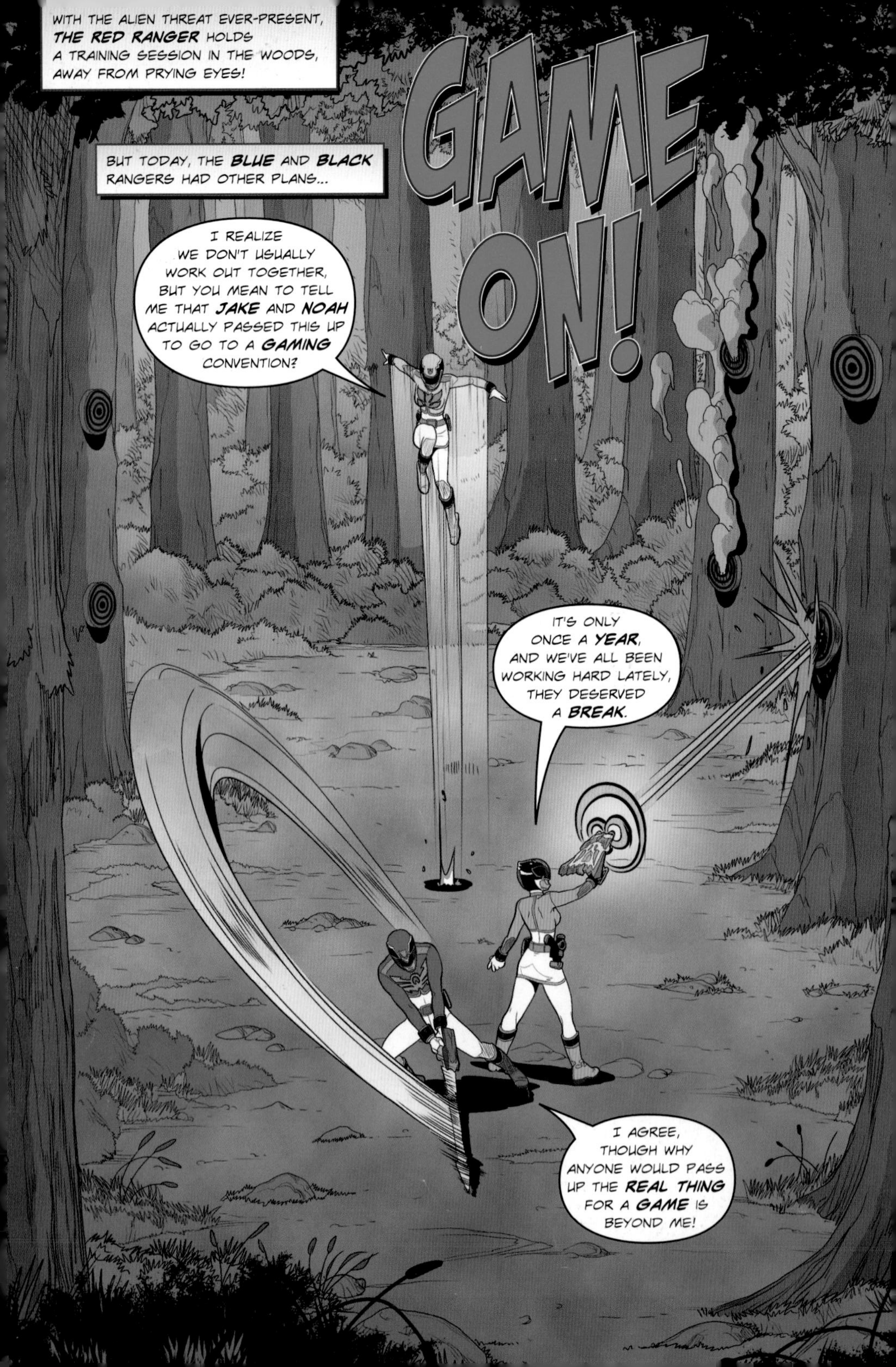
WITH THE ALIEN THREAT EVER-PRESENT, THE RED RANGER HOLDS A TRAINING SESSION IN THE WOODS, AWAY FROM PRYING EYES!
BUT TODAY, THE BLUE AND BLACK RANGERS HAD OTHER PLANS...
GAME ON!
I REALIZE WE DON'T USUALLY WORK OUT TOGETHER, BUT YOU MEAN TO TELL ME THAT JAKE AND NOAH ACTUALLY PASSED THIS UP TO GO TO A GAMING CONVENTION?
IT'S ONLY ONCE A YEAR, AND WE'VE ALL BEEN WORKING HARD LATELY, THEY DESERVED A BREAK.
I AGREE, THOUGH WHY ANYONE WOULD PASS UP THE REAL THING FOR A GAME IS BEYOND ME!

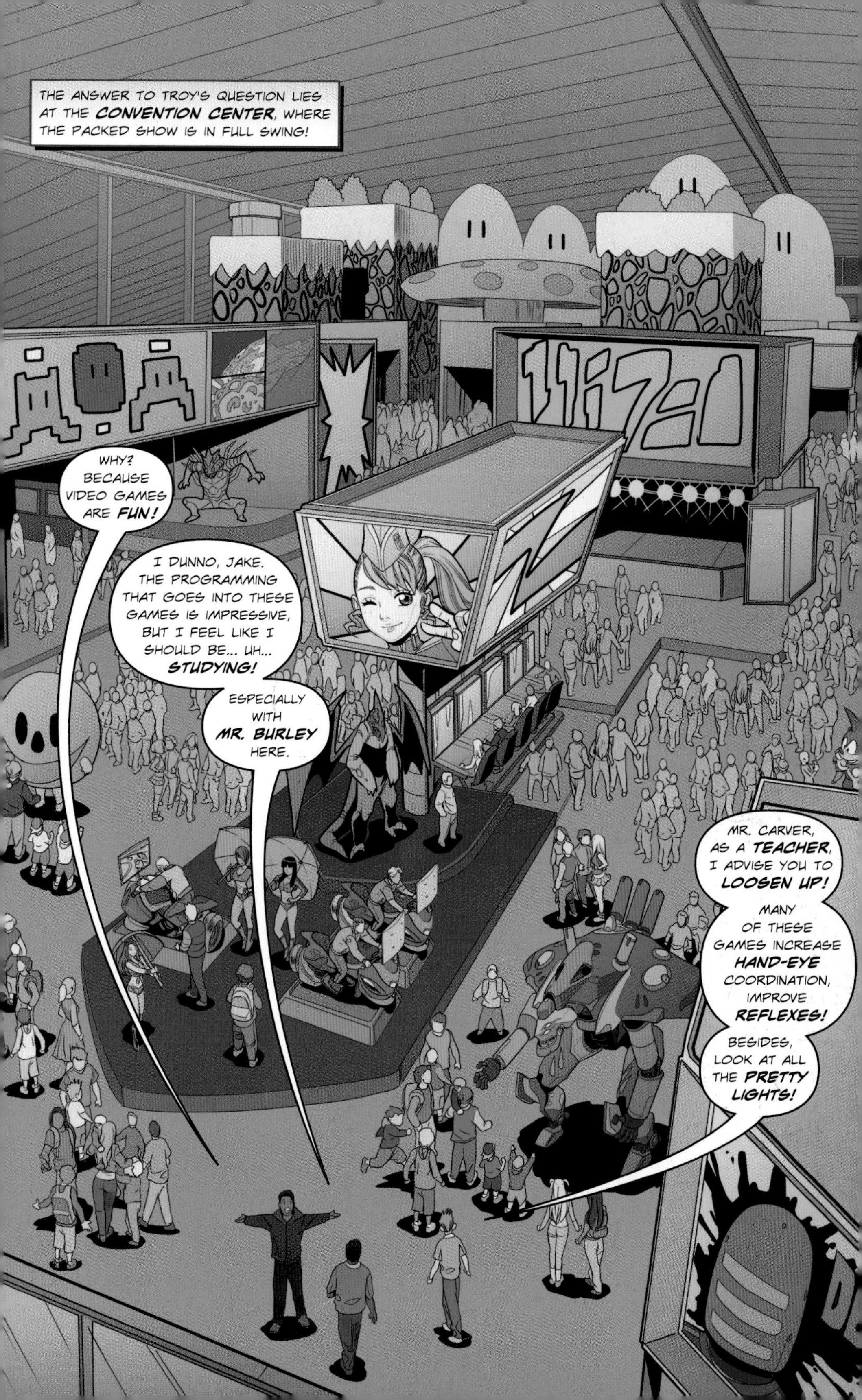
THE ANSWER TO TROY'S QUESTION LIES AT THE CONVENTION CENTER, WHERE THE PACKED SHOW IS IN FULL SWING!
WHY? BECAUSE VIDEO GAMES ARE FUN!
I DUNNO, JAKE. THE PROGRAMMING THAT GOES INTO THESE GAMES IS IMPRESSIVE, BUT I FEEL LIKE I SHOULD BE... UH... STUDYING!
ESPECIALLY WITH MR. BURLEY HERE.
MR. CARVER, AS A TEACHER, I ADVISE YOU TO LOOSEN UP!
MANY OF THESE GAMES INCREASE HAND-EYE COORDINATION, IMPROVE REFLEXES!
BESIDES, LOOK AT ALL THE PRETTY LIGHTS!

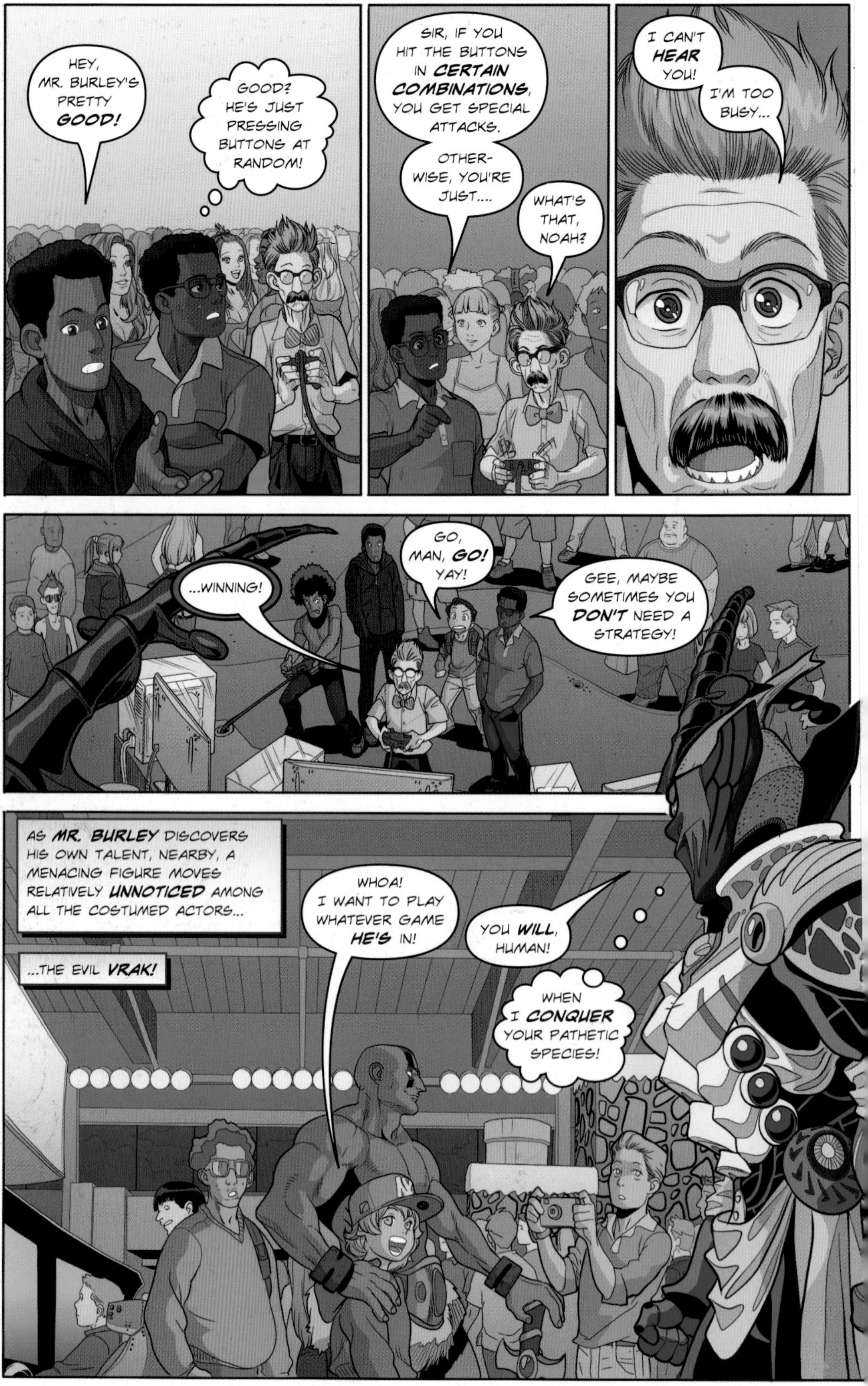
HEY, MR. BURLEY'S PRETTY **GOOD!**
GOOD? HE'S JUST PRESSING BUTTONS AT RANDOM!
SIR, IF YOU HIT THE BUTTONS IN **CERTAIN COMBINATIONS**, YOU GET SPECIAL ATTACKS.
OTHER-WISE, YOU'RE JUST....
WHAT'S THAT, NOAH?
I CAN'T **HEAR** YOU!
I'M TOO BUSY...
...WINNING!
GO, MAN, **GO!** YAY!
GEE, MAYBE SOMETIMES YOU **DON'T** NEED A STRATEGY!
AS **MR. BURLEY** DISCOVERS HIS OWN TALENT, NEARBY, A MENACING FIGURE MOVES RELATIVELY **UNNOTICED** AMONG ALL THE COSTUMED ACTORS...
...THE EVIL **VRAK!**
WHOA! I WANT TO PLAY WHATEVER GAME **HE'S** IN!
YOU **WILL**, HUMAN!
WHEN I **CONQUER** YOUR PATHETIC SPECIES!

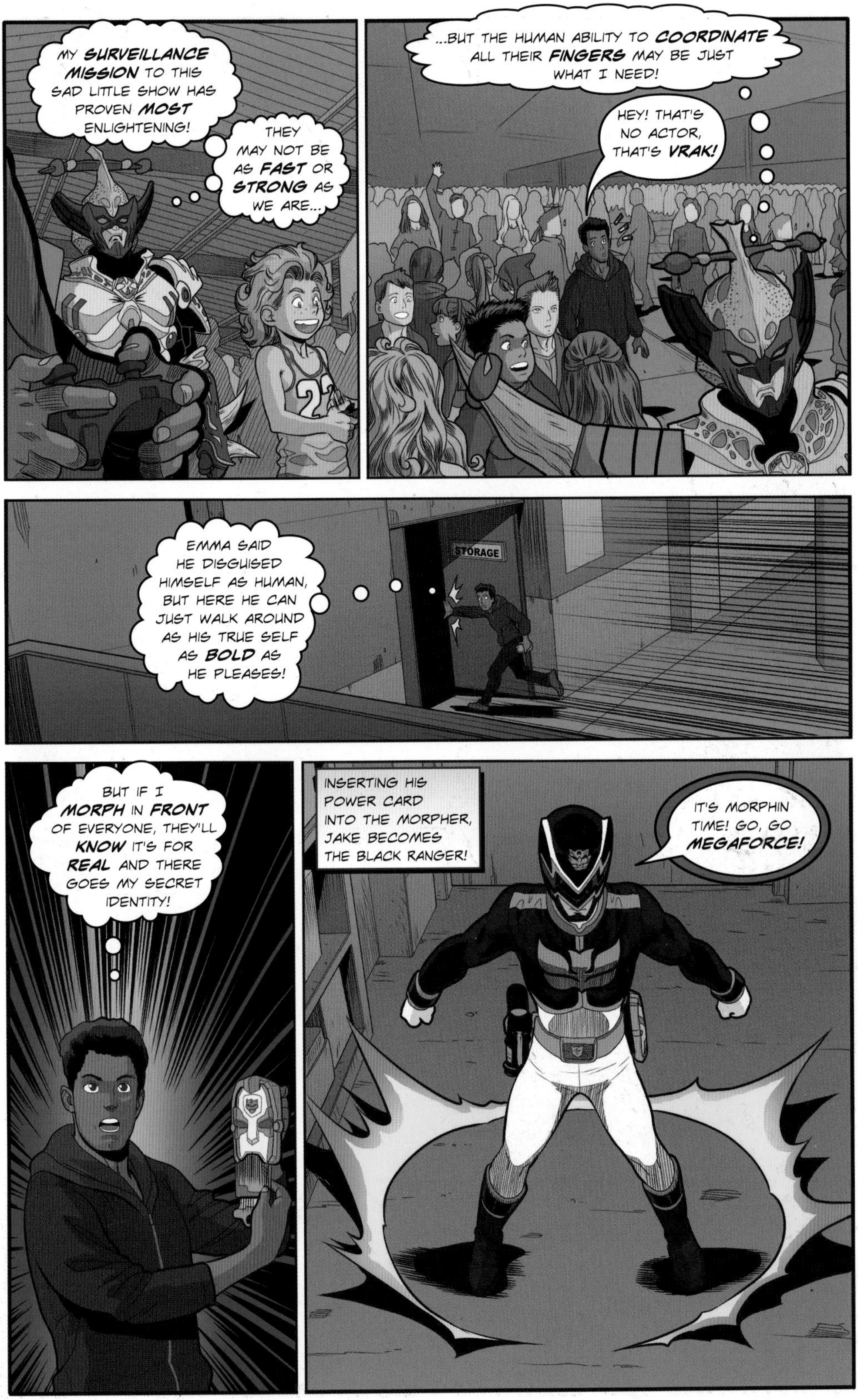
MY SURVEILLANCE MISSION TO THIS SAD LITTLE SHOW HAS PROVEN MOST ENLIGHTENING!
THEY MAY NOT BE AS FAST OR STRONG AS WE ARE...
...BUT THE HUMAN ABILITY TO COORDINATE ALL THEIR FINGERS MAY BE JUST WHAT I NEED!
HEY! THAT'S NO ACTOR, THAT'S VRAK!
EMMA SAID HE DISGUISED HIMSELF AS HUMAN, BUT HERE HE CAN JUST WALK AROUND AS HIS TRUE SELF AS BOLD AS HE PLEASES!
STORAGE
BUT IF I MORPH IN FRONT OF EVERYONE, THEY'LL KNOW IT'S FOR REAL AND THERE GOES MY SECRET IDENTITY!
INSERTING HIS POWER CARD INTO THE MORPHER, JAKE BECOMES THE BLACK RANGER!
IT'S MORPHIN TIME! GO, GO MEGAFORCE!

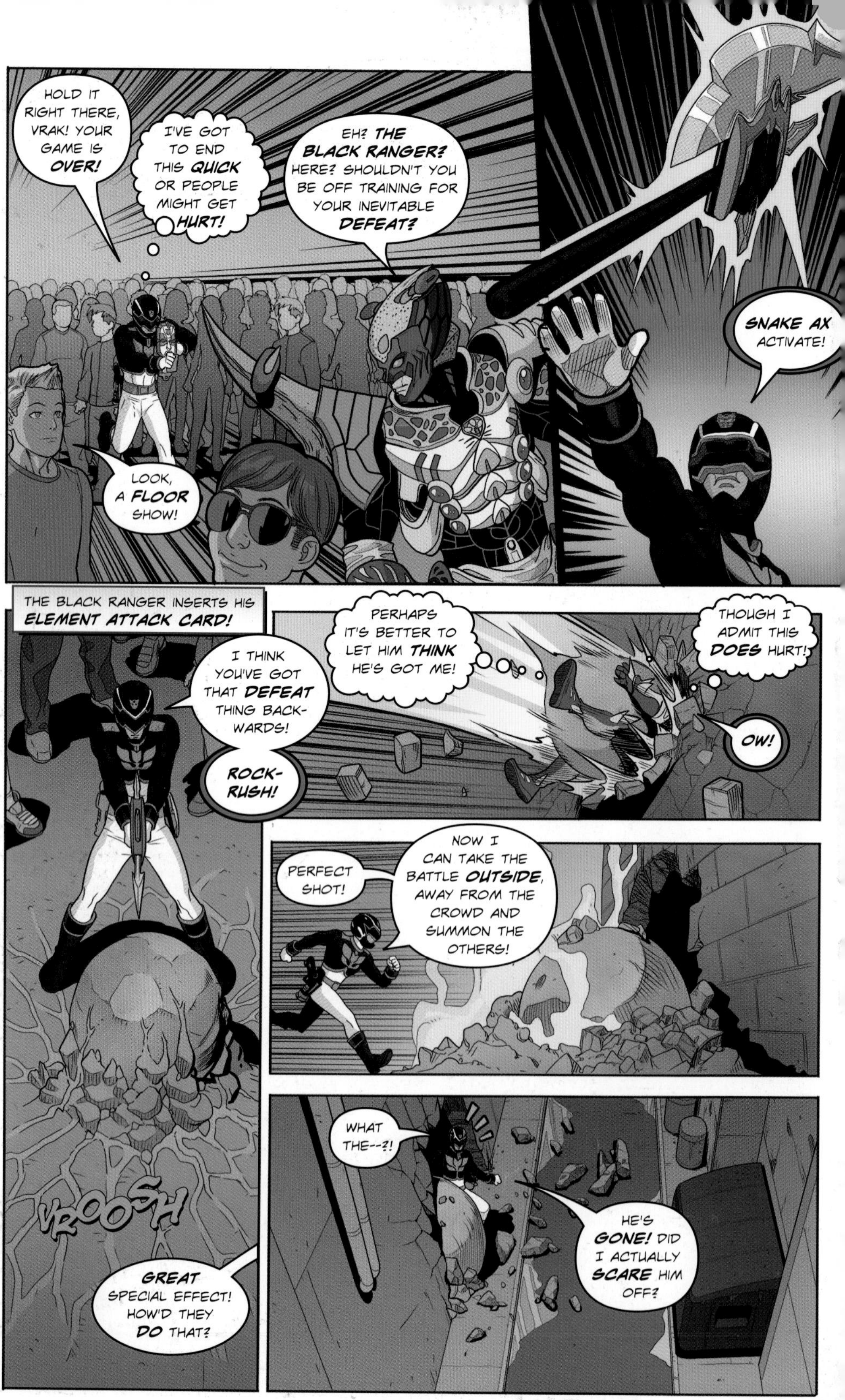
HOLD IT RIGHT THERE, VRAK! YOUR GAME IS OVER!
I'VE GOT TO END THIS QUICK OR PEOPLE MIGHT GET HURT!
EH? THE BLACK RANGER? HERE? SHOULDN'T YOU BE OFF TRAINING FOR YOUR INEVITABLE DEFEAT?
LOOK, A FLOOR SHOW!
SNAKE AX ACTIVATE!
THE BLACK RANGER INSERTS HIS ELEMENT ATTACK CARD!
I THINK YOU'VE GOT THAT DEFEAT THING BACK-WARDS!
ROCK-RUSH!
VROOSH
GREAT SPECIAL EFFECT! HOW'D THEY DO THAT?
PERHAPS IT'S BETTER TO LET HIM THINK HE'S GOT ME!
THOUGH I ADMIT THIS DOES HURT!
OW!
PERFECT SHOT!
NOW I CAN TAKE THE BATTLE OUTSIDE, AWAY FROM THE CROWD AND SUMMON THE OTHERS!
WHAT THE--?!
HE'S GONE! DID I ACTUALLY SCARE HIM OFF?

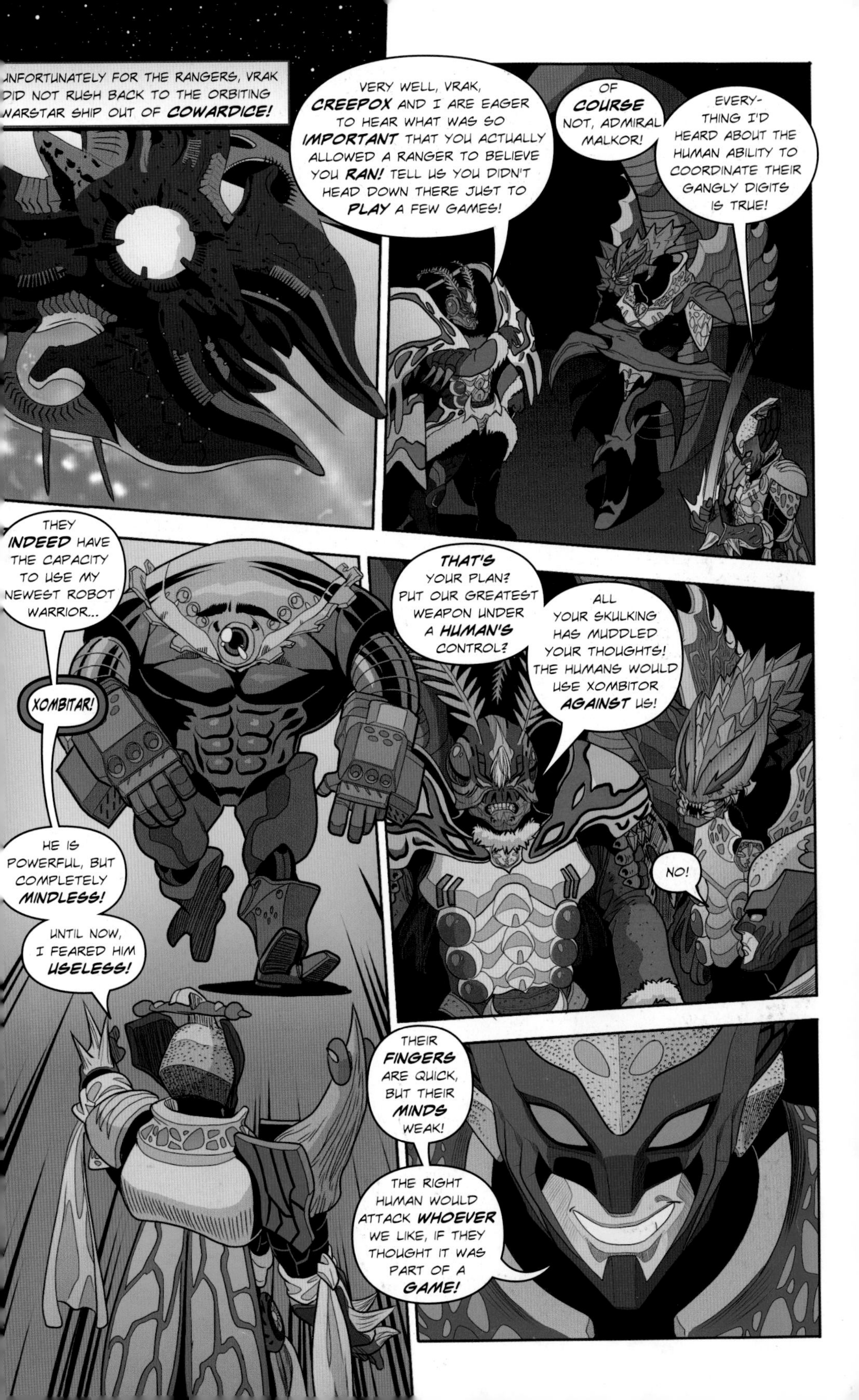
UNFORTUNATELY FOR THE RANGERS, VRAK DID NOT RUSH BACK TO THE ORBITING WARSTAR SHIP OUT OF COWARDICE!
VERY WELL, VRAK, CREEPOX AND I ARE EAGER TO HEAR WHAT WAS SO IMPORTANT THAT YOU ACTUALLY ALLOWED A RANGER TO BELIEVE YOU RAN! TELL US YOU DIDN'T HEAD DOWN THERE JUST TO PLAY A FEW GAMES!
OF COURSE NOT, ADMIRAL MALKOR!
EVERY-THING I'D HEARD ABOUT THE HUMAN ABILITY TO COORDINATE THEIR GANGLY DIGITS IS TRUE!
THEY INDEED HAVE THE CAPACITY TO USE MY NEWEST ROBOT WARRIOR...
XOMBITAR!
HE IS POWERFUL, BUT COMPLETELY MINDLESS!
UNTIL NOW, I FEARED HIM USELESS!
THAT'S YOUR PLAN? PUT OUR GREATEST WEAPON UNDER A HUMAN'S CONTROL?
ALL YOUR SKULKING HAS MUDDLED YOUR THOUGHTS! THE HUMANS WOULD USE XOMBITOR AGAINST US!
NO!
THEIR FINGERS ARE QUICK, BUT THEIR MINDS WEAK!
THE RIGHT HUMAN WOULD ATTACK WHOEVER WE LIKE, IF THEY THOUGHT IT WAS PART OF A GAME!

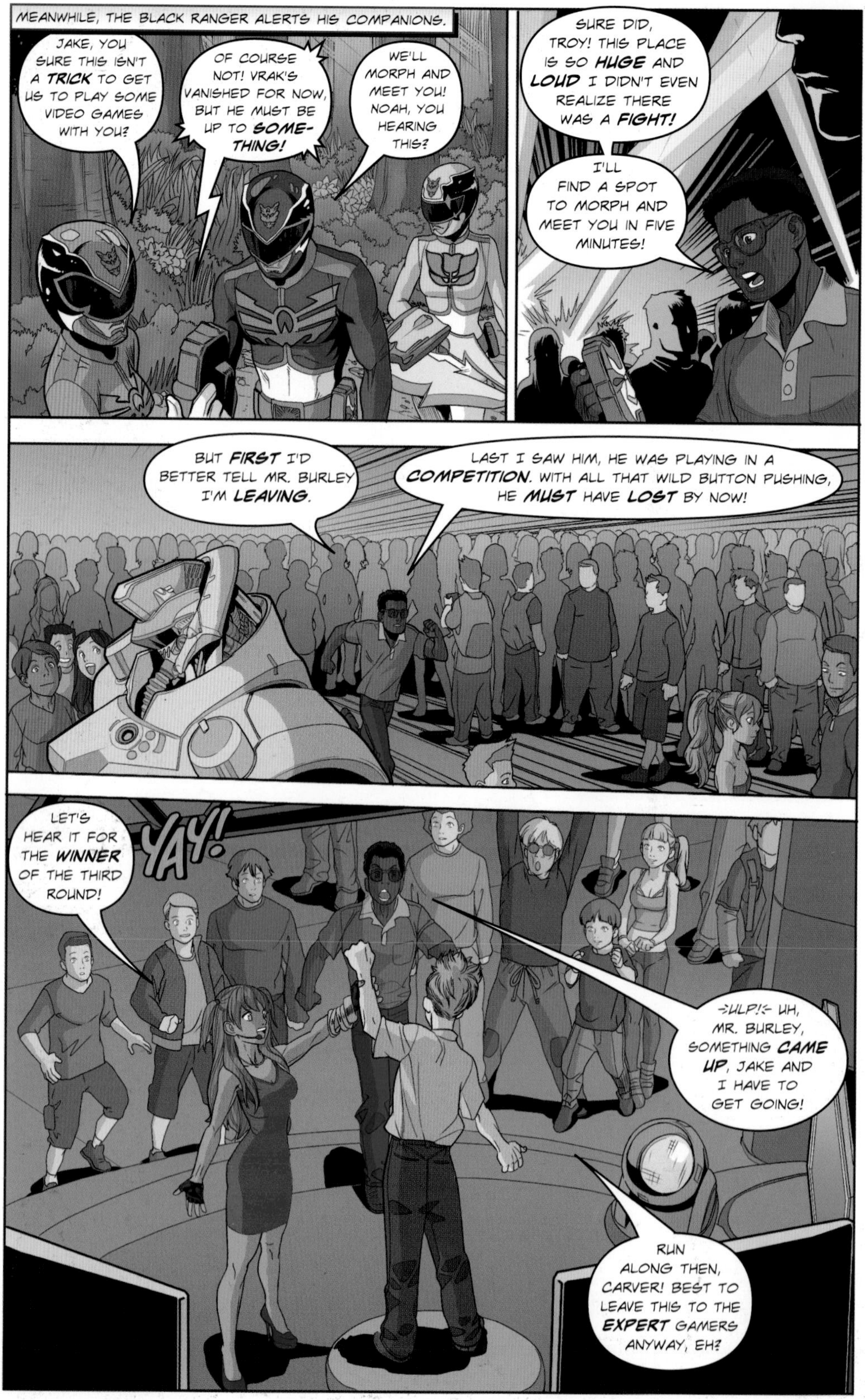
MEANWHILE, THE BLACK RANGER ALERTS HIS COMPANIONS.
JAKE, YOU SURE THIS ISN'T A TRICK TO GET US TO PLAY SOME VIDEO GAMES WITH YOU?
OF COURSE NOT! VRAK'S VANISHED FOR NOW, BUT HE MUST BE UP TO SOME-THING!
WE'LL MORPH AND MEET YOU! NOAH, YOU HEARING THIS?
SURE DID, TROY! THIS PLACE IS SO HUGE AND LOUD I DIDN'T EVEN REALIZE THERE WAS A FIGHT!
I'LL FIND A SPOT TO MORPH AND MEET YOU IN FIVE MINUTES!
BUT FIRST I'D BETTER TELL MR. BURLEY I'M LEAVING.
LAST I SAW HIM, HE WAS PLAYING IN A COMPETITION. WITH ALL THAT WILD BUTTON PUSHING, HE MUST HAVE LOST BY NOW!
LET'S HEAR IT FOR THE WINNER OF THE THIRD ROUND!
YAY!
=ULP!= UH, MR. BURLEY, SOMETHING CAME UP, JAKE AND I HAVE TO GET GOING!
RUN ALONG THEN, CARVER! BEST TO LEAVE THIS TO THE EXPERT GAMERS ANYWAY, EH?

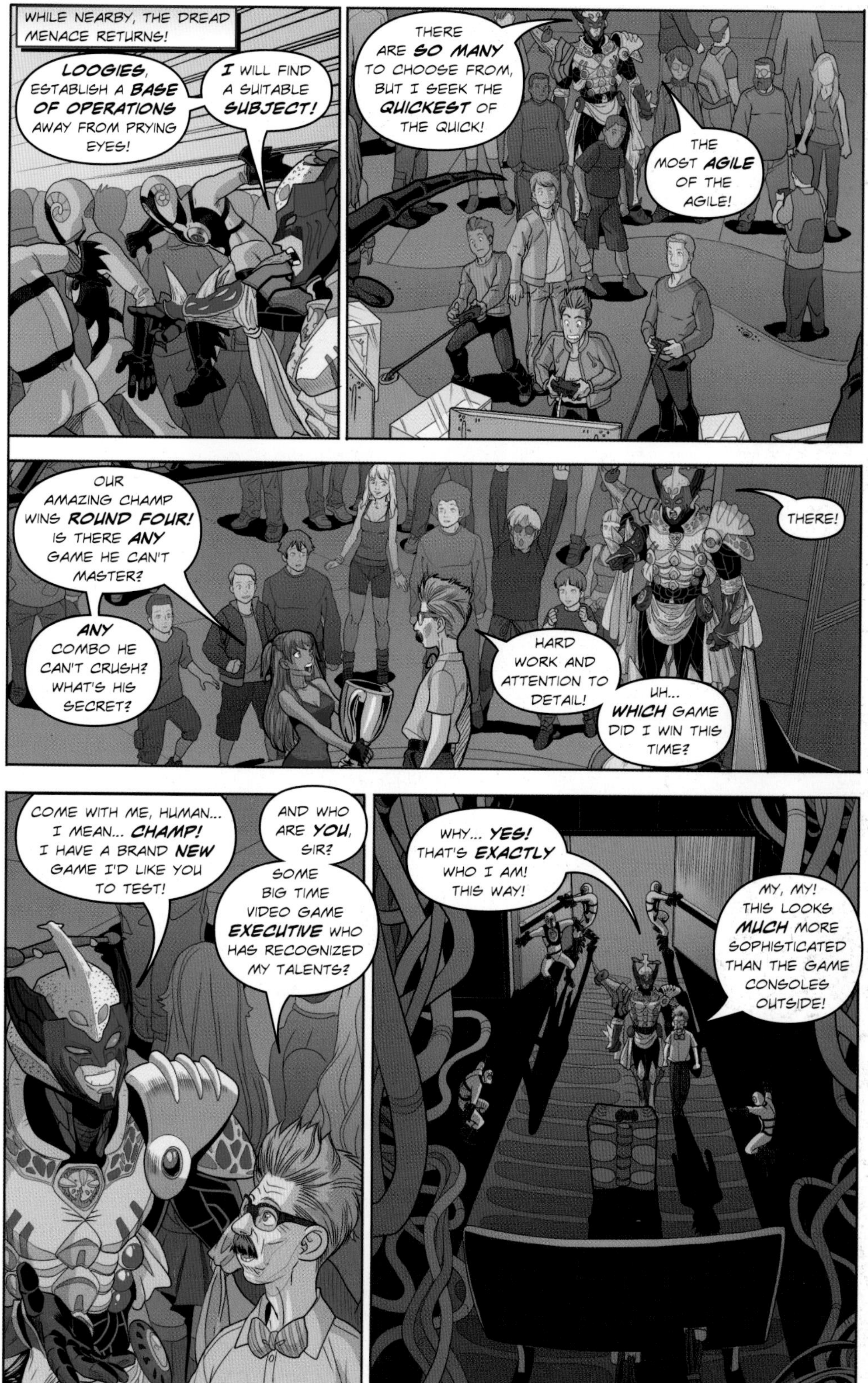

WHILE NEARBY, THE DREAD MENACE RETURNS!
LOOGIES, ESTABLISH A BASE OF OPERATIONS AWAY FROM PRYING EYES!
I WILL FIND A SUITABLE SUBJECT!
THERE ARE SO MANY TO CHOOSE FROM, BUT I SEEK THE QUICKEST OF THE QUICK!
THE MOST AGILE OF THE AGILE!
OUR AMAZING CHAMP WINS ROUND FOUR! IS THERE ANY GAME HE CAN'T MASTER?
ANY COMBO HE CAN'T CRUSH? WHAT'S HIS SECRET?
HARD WORK AND ATTENTION TO DETAIL!
UH... WHICH GAME DID I WIN THIS TIME?
THERE!
COME WITH ME, HUMAN... I MEAN... CHAMP! I HAVE A BRAND NEW GAME I'D LIKE YOU TO TEST!
AND WHO ARE YOU, SIR?
SOME BIG TIME VIDEO GAME EXECUTIVE WHO HAS RECOGNIZED MY TALENTS?
WHY... YES! THAT'S EXACTLY WHO I AM! THIS WAY!
MY, MY! THIS LOOKS MUCH MORE SOPHISTICATED THAN THE GAME CONSOLES OUTSIDE!

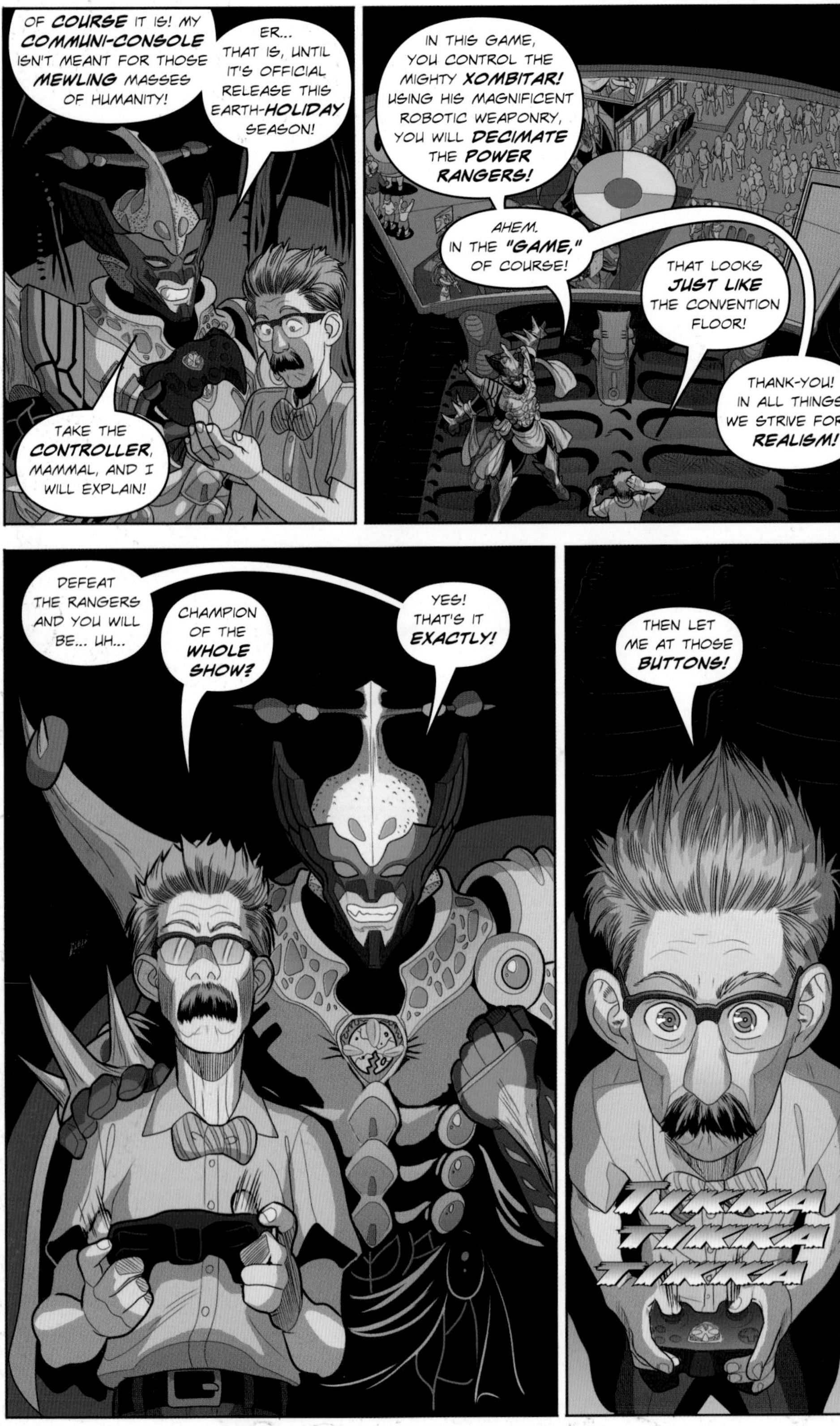
OF COURSE IT IS! MY COMMUNI-CONSOLE ISN'T MEANT FOR THOSE MEWLING MASSES OF HUMANITY!
ER... THAT IS, UNTIL IT'S OFFICIAL RELEASE THIS EARTH-HOLIDAY SEASON!
TAKE THE CONTROLLER, MAMMAL, AND I WILL EXPLAIN!
IN THIS GAME, YOU CONTROL THE MIGHTY XOMBITAR! USING HIS MAGNIFICENT ROBOTIC WEAPONRY, YOU WILL DECIMATE THE POWER RANGERS!
AHEM. IN THE "GAME," OF COURSE!
THAT LOOKS JUST LIKE THE CONVENTION FLOOR!
THANK-YOU! IN ALL THINGS WE STRIVE FOR... REALISM!
DEFEAT THE RANGERS AND YOU WILL BE... UH...
CHAMPION OF THE WHOLE SHOW?
YES! THAT'S IT EXACTLY!
THEN LET ME AT THOSE BUTTONS!
TIKKA TIKKA TIKKA

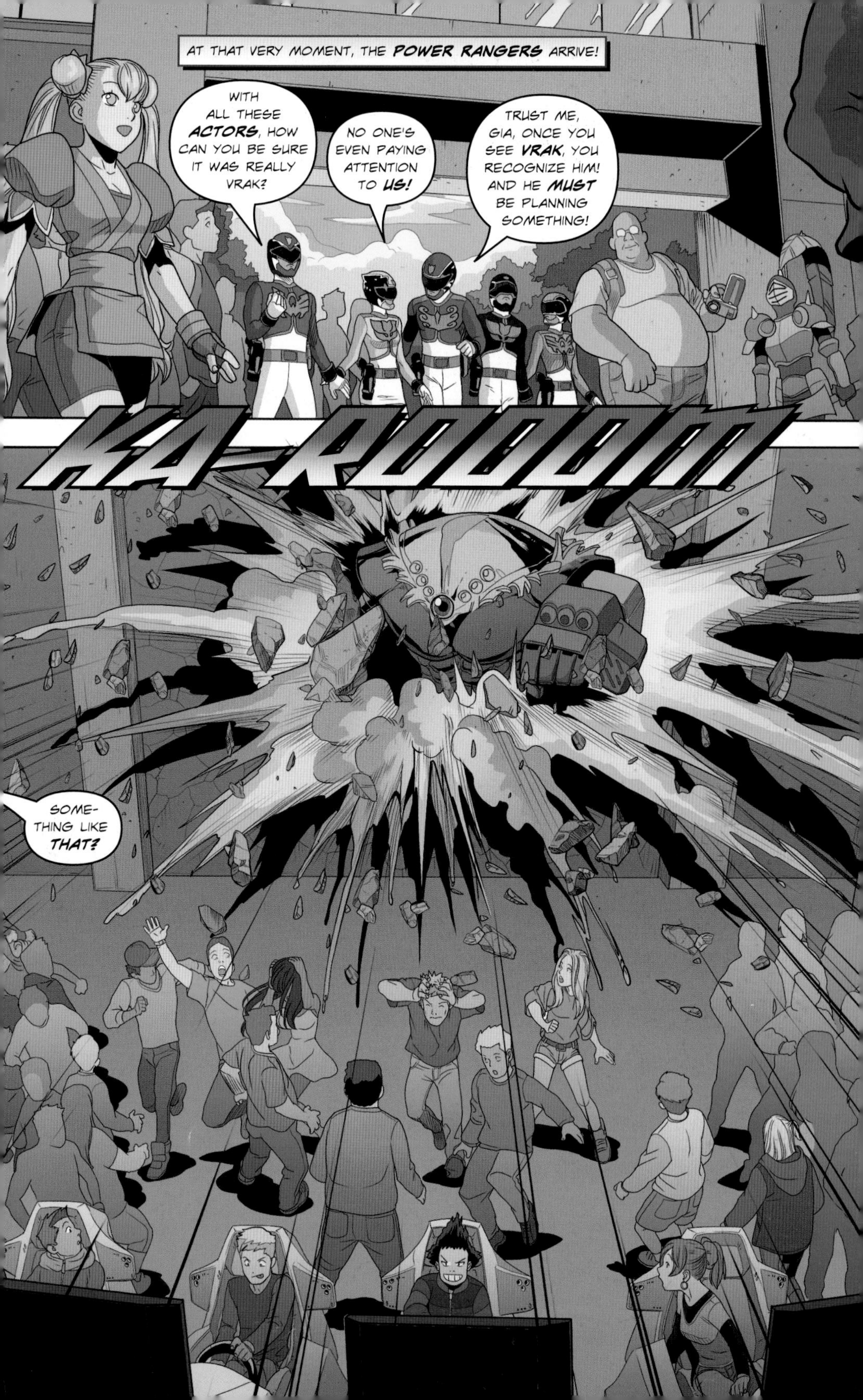
AT THAT VERY MOMENT, THE POWER RANGERS ARRIVE!
WITH ALL THESE ACTORS, HOW CAN YOU BE SURE IT WAS REALLY VRAK?
NO ONE'S EVEN PAYING ATTENTION TO US!
TRUST ME, GIA, ONCE YOU SEE VRAK, YOU RECOGNIZE HIM! AND HE MUST BE PLANNING SOMETHING!
KA-ROOOM
SOME-THING LIKE THAT?

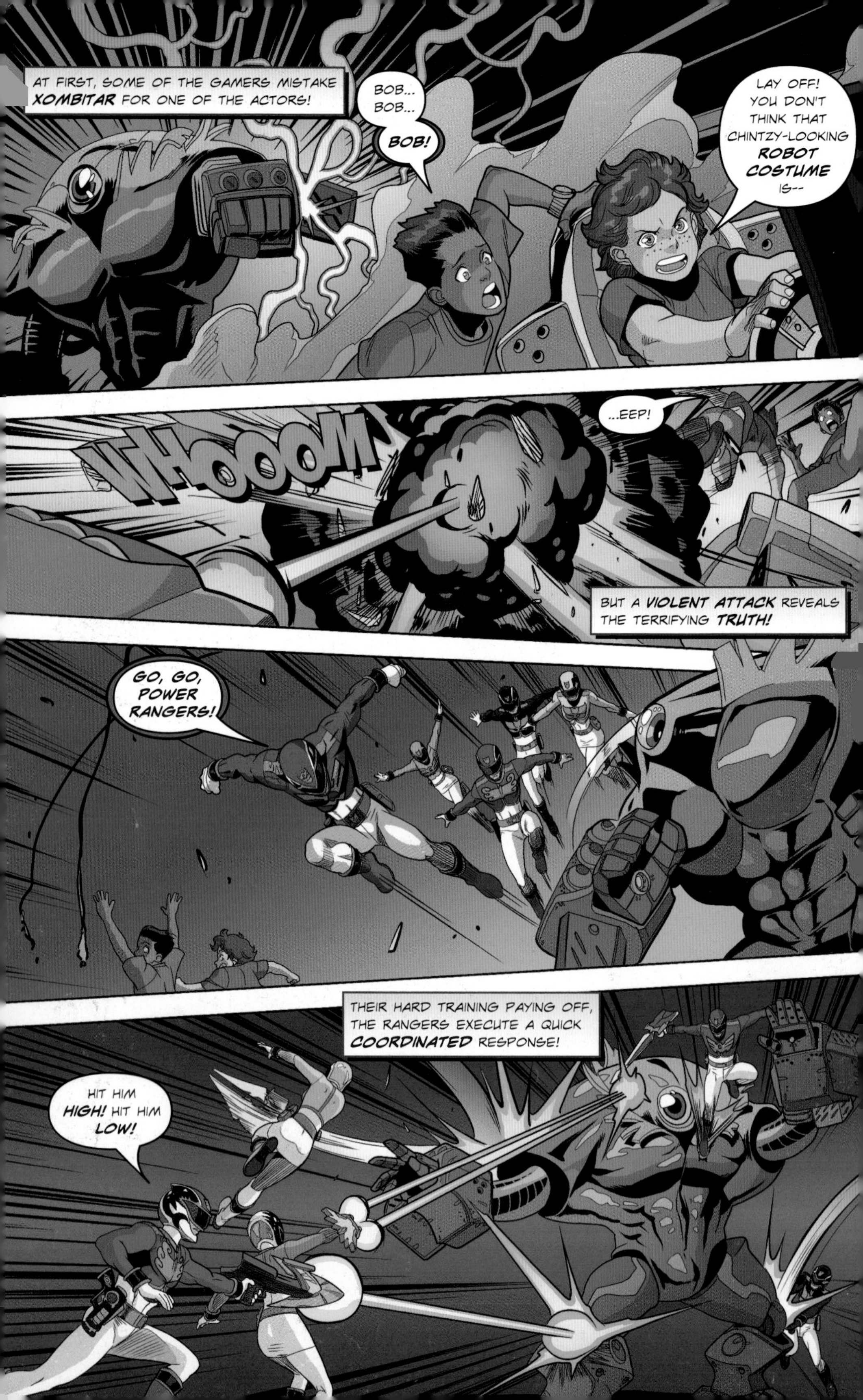
AT FIRST, SOME OF THE GAMERS MISTAKE XOMBITAR FOR ONE OF THE ACTORS!
BOB... BOB... BOB!
LAY OFF! YOU DON'T THINK THAT CHINTZY-LOOKING ROBOT COSTUME IS--
WHOOOM
...EEP!
BUT A VIOLENT ATTACK REVEALS THE TERRIFYING TRUTH!
GO, GO, POWER RANGERS!
THEIR HARD TRAINING PAYING OFF, THE RANGERS EXECUTE A QUICK COORDINATED RESPONSE!
HIT HIM HIGH! HIT HIM LOW!

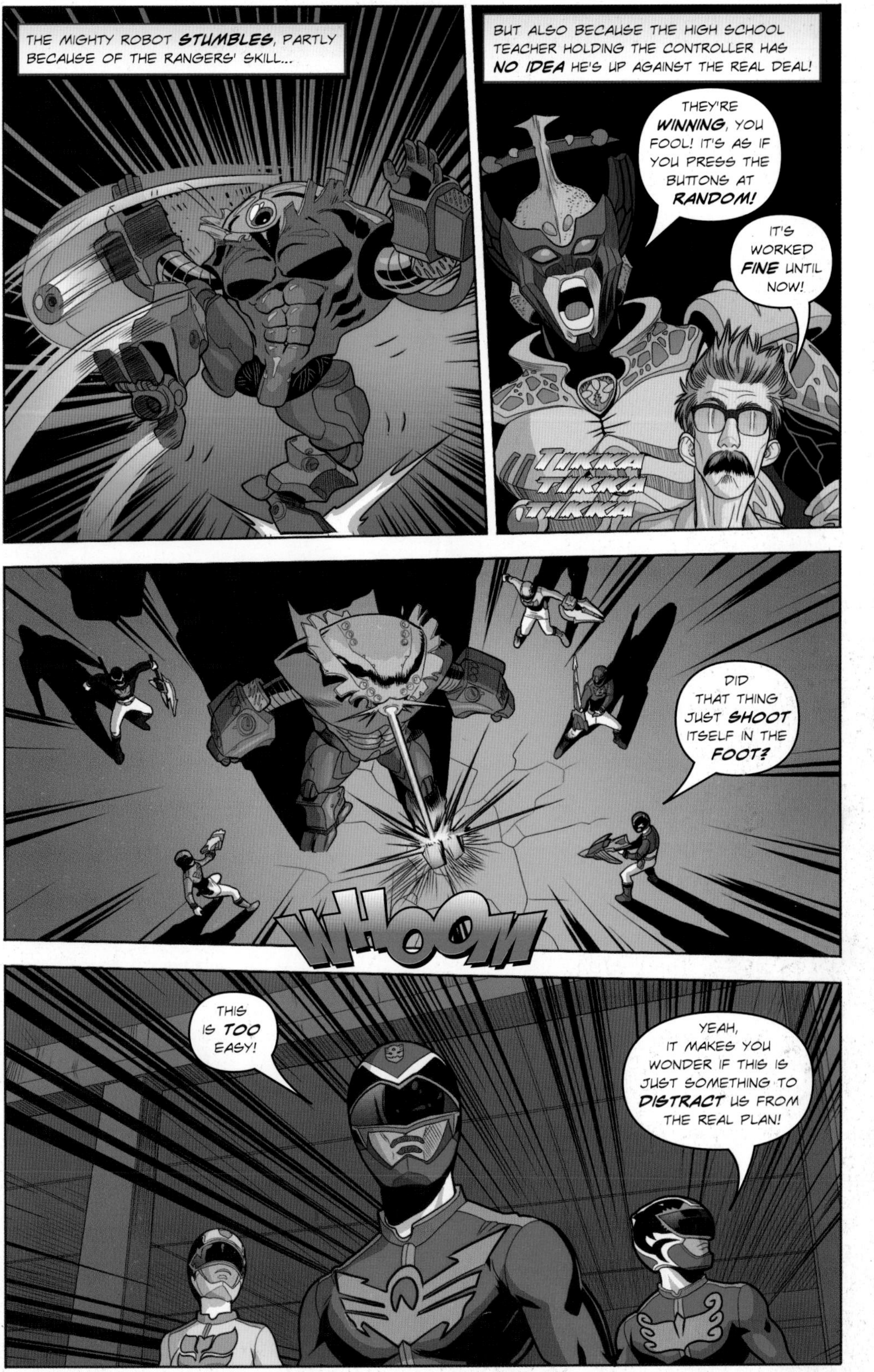
THE MIGHTY ROBOT STUMBLES, PARTLY BECAUSE OF THE RANGERS' SKILL...
BUT ALSO BECAUSE THE HIGH SCHOOL TEACHER HOLDING THE CONTROLLER HAS NO IDEA HE'S UP AGAINST THE REAL DEAL!
THEY'RE WINNING, YOU FOOL! IT'S AS IF YOU PRESS THE BUTTONS AT RANDOM!
IT'S WORKED FINE UNTIL NOW!
TIKKA TIKKA TIKKA
DID THAT THING JUST SHOOT ITSELF IN THE FOOT?
WHOOM
THIS IS TOO EASY!
YEAH, IT MAKES YOU WONDER IF THIS IS JUST SOMETHING TO DISTRACT US FROM THE REAL PLAN!

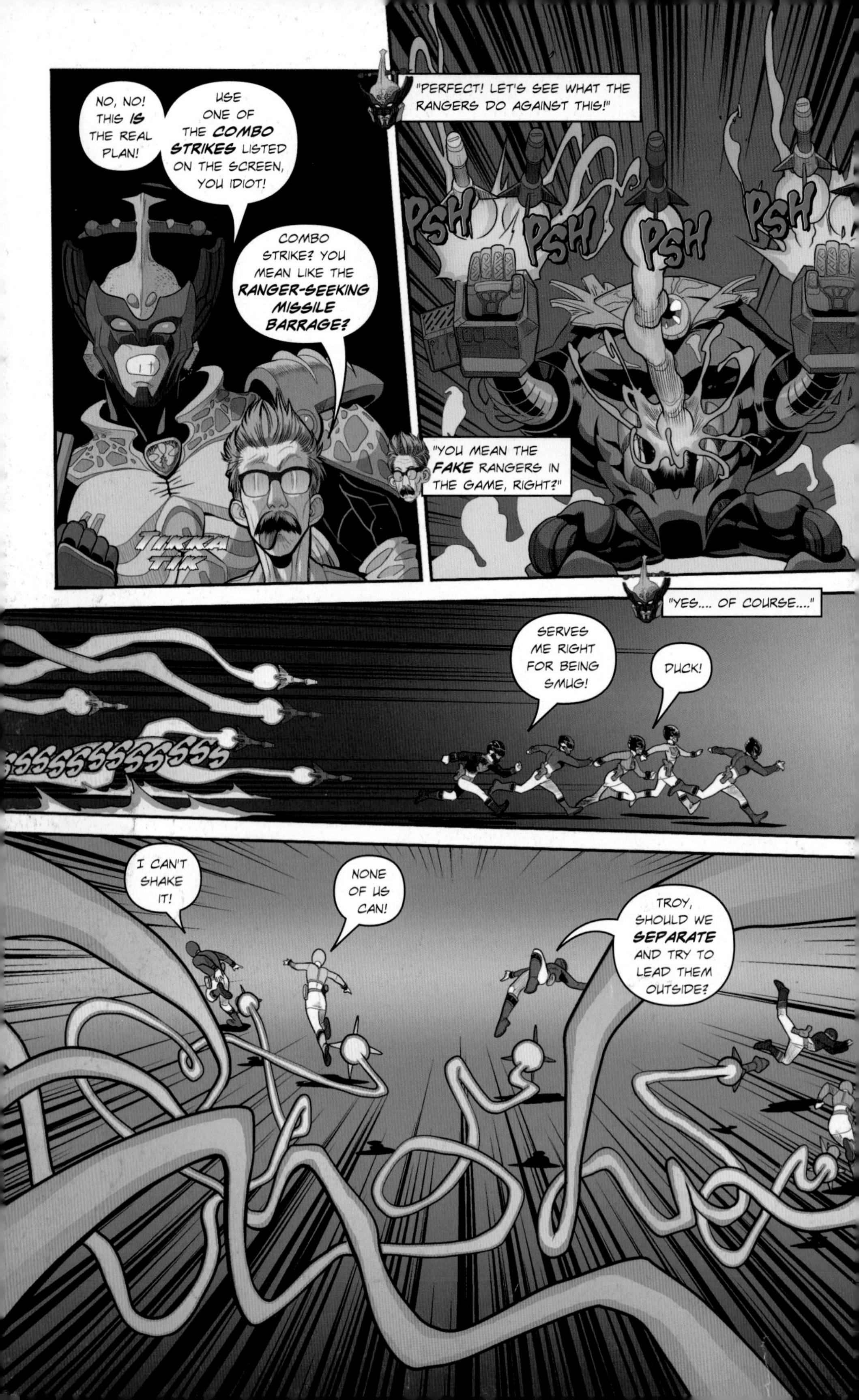
NO, NO! THIS IS THE REAL PLAN!
USE ONE OF THE COMBO STRIKES LISTED ON THE SCREEN, YOU IDIOT!
COMBO STRIKE? YOU MEAN LIKE THE RANGER-SEEKING MISSILE BARRAGE?
TIKKA TIK
"PERFECT! LET'S SEE WHAT THE RANGERS DO AGAINST THIS!"
PSH PSH PSH PSH
"YOU MEAN THE FAKE RANGERS IN THE GAME, RIGHT?"
"YES.... OF COURSE...."
SSSSSSSSSSSSS
SERVES ME RIGHT FOR BEING SMUG!
DUCK!
I CAN'T SHAKE IT!
NONE OF US CAN!
TROY, SHOULD WE SEPARATE AND TRY TO LEAD THEM OUTSIDE?

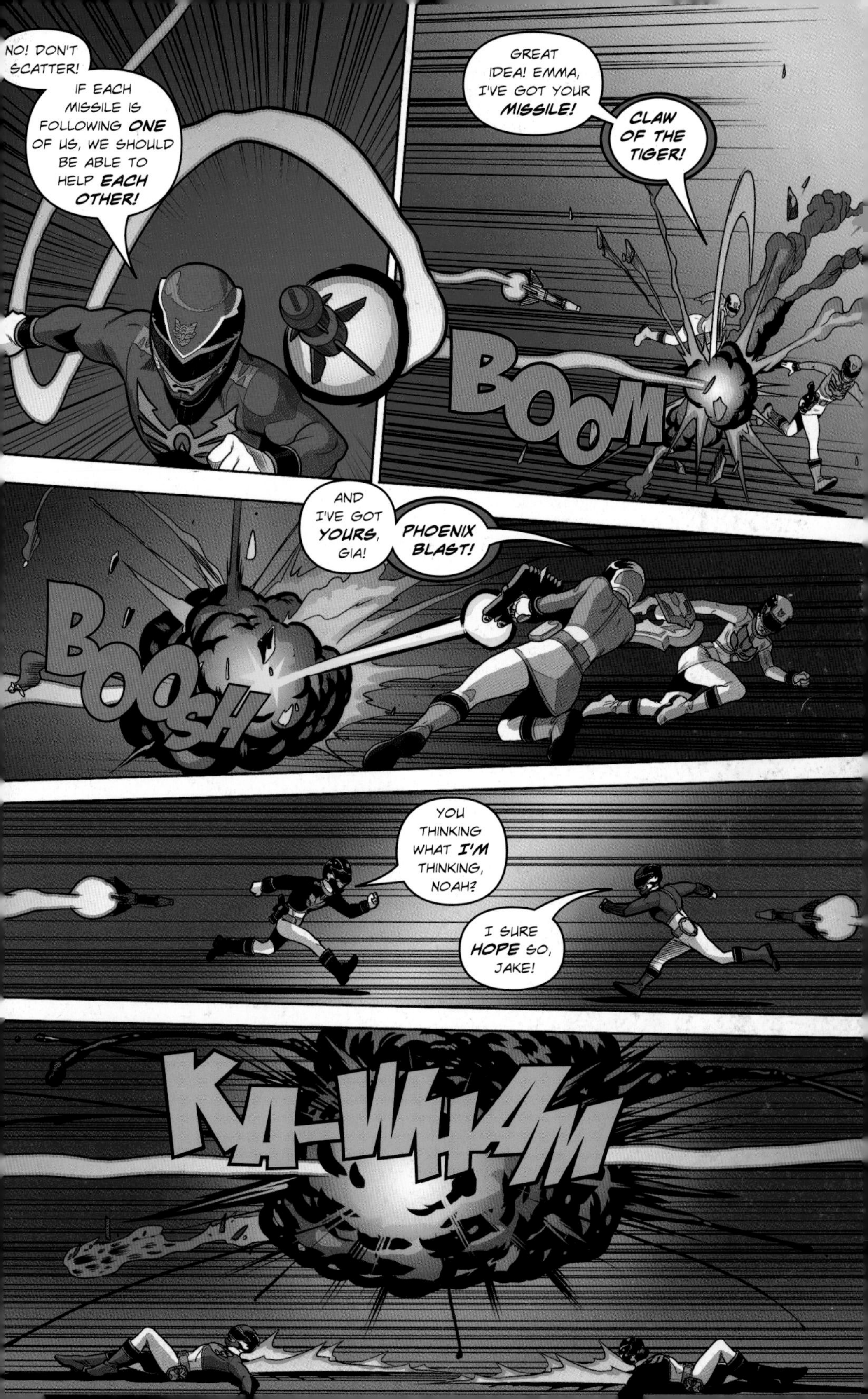
NO! DON'T SCATTER!
IF EACH MISSILE IS FOLLOWING ONE OF US, WE SHOULD BE ABLE TO HELP EACH OTHER!
GREAT IDEA! EMMA, I'VE GOT YOUR MISSILE!
CLAW OF THE TIGER!
BOOM
AND I'VE GOT YOURS, GIA!
PHOENIX BLAST!
BOOSH
YOU THINKING WHAT I'M THINKING, NOAH?
I SURE HOPE SO, JAKE!
KA-WHAM

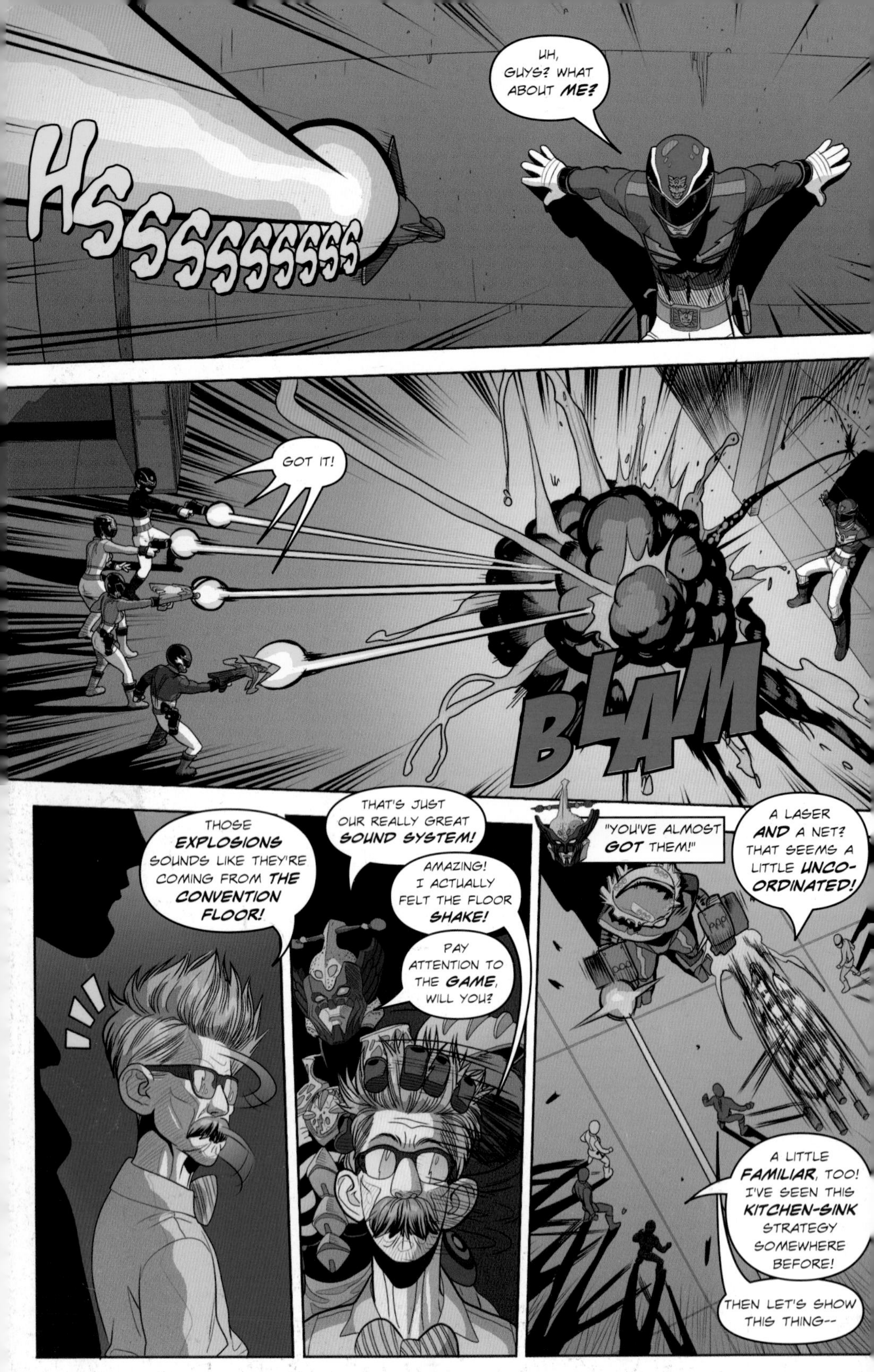

UH, GUYS? WHAT ABOUT ME?
HSSSSSSSSSS
GOT IT!
BLAM
THOSE EXPLOSIONS SOUNDS LIKE THEY'RE COMING FROM THE CONVENTION FLOOR!
THAT'S JUST OUR REALLY GREAT SOUND SYSTEM!
AMAZING! I ACTUALLY FELT THE FLOOR SHAKE!
PAY ATTENTION TO THE GAME, WILL YOU?
"YOU'VE ALMOST GOT THEM!"
A LASER AND A NET? THAT SEEMS A LITTLE UNCO-ORDINATED!
A LITTLE FAMILIAR, TOO! I'VE SEEN THIS KITCHEN-SINK STRATEGY SOMEWHERE BEFORE!
THEN LET'S SHOW THIS THING--

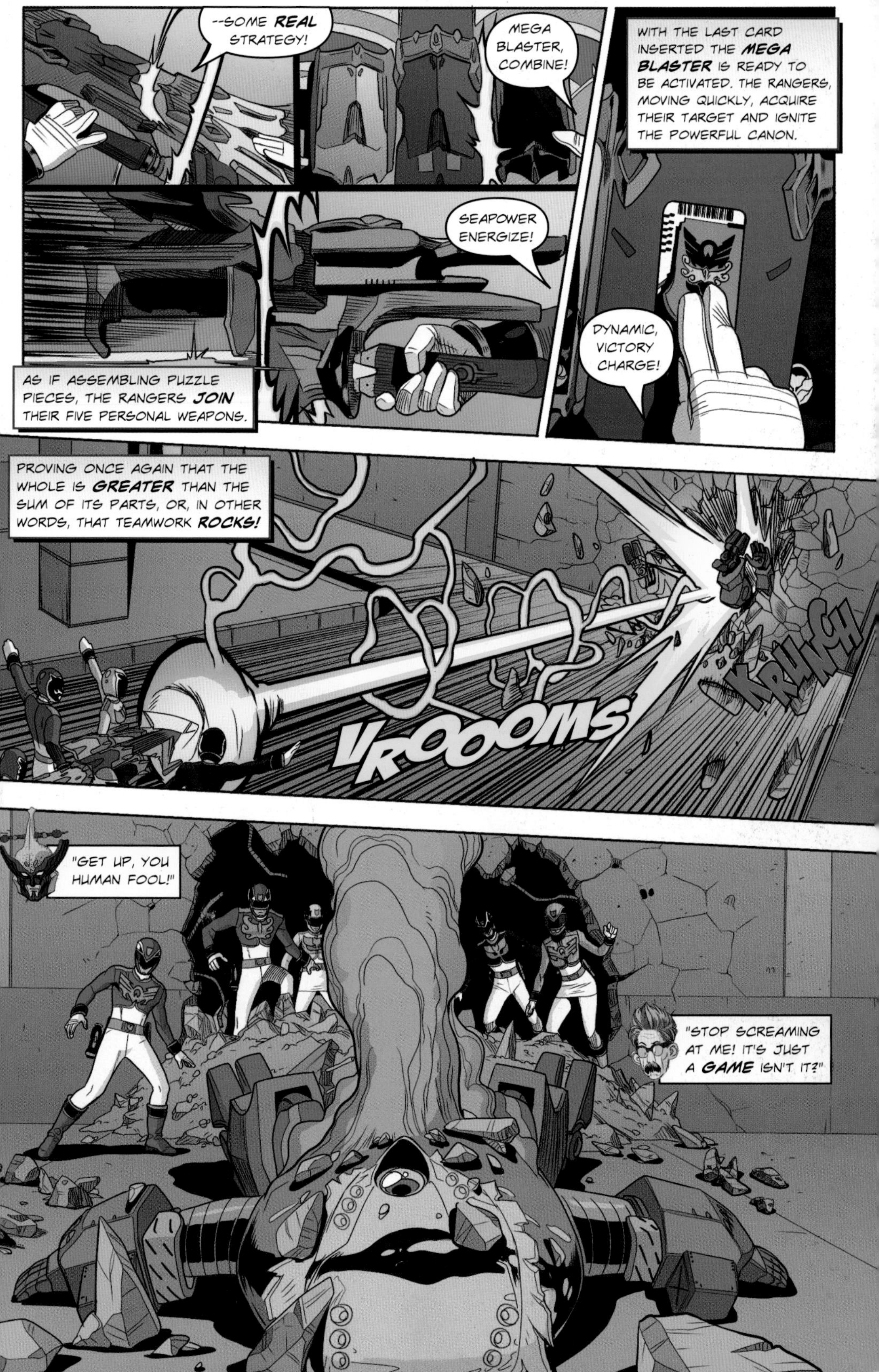
--SOME REAL STRATEGY!
MEGA BLASTER, COMBINE!
WITH THE LAST CARD INSERTED THE MEGA BLASTER IS READY TO BE ACTIVATED. THE RANGERS, MOVING QUICKLY, ACQUIRE THEIR TARGET AND IGNITE THE POWERFUL CANON.
SEAPOWER ENERGIZE!
DYNAMIC, VICTORY CHARGE!
AS IF ASSEMBLING PUZZLE PIECES, THE RANGERS JOIN THEIR FIVE PERSONAL WEAPONS.
PROVING ONCE AGAIN THAT THE WHOLE IS GREATER THAN THE SUM OF ITS PARTS, OR, IN OTHER WORDS, THAT TEAMWORK ROCKS!
KRUNCH
VROOOMS
"GET UP, YOU HUMAN FOOL!"
"STOP SCREAMING AT ME! IT'S JUST A GAME ISN'T IT?"

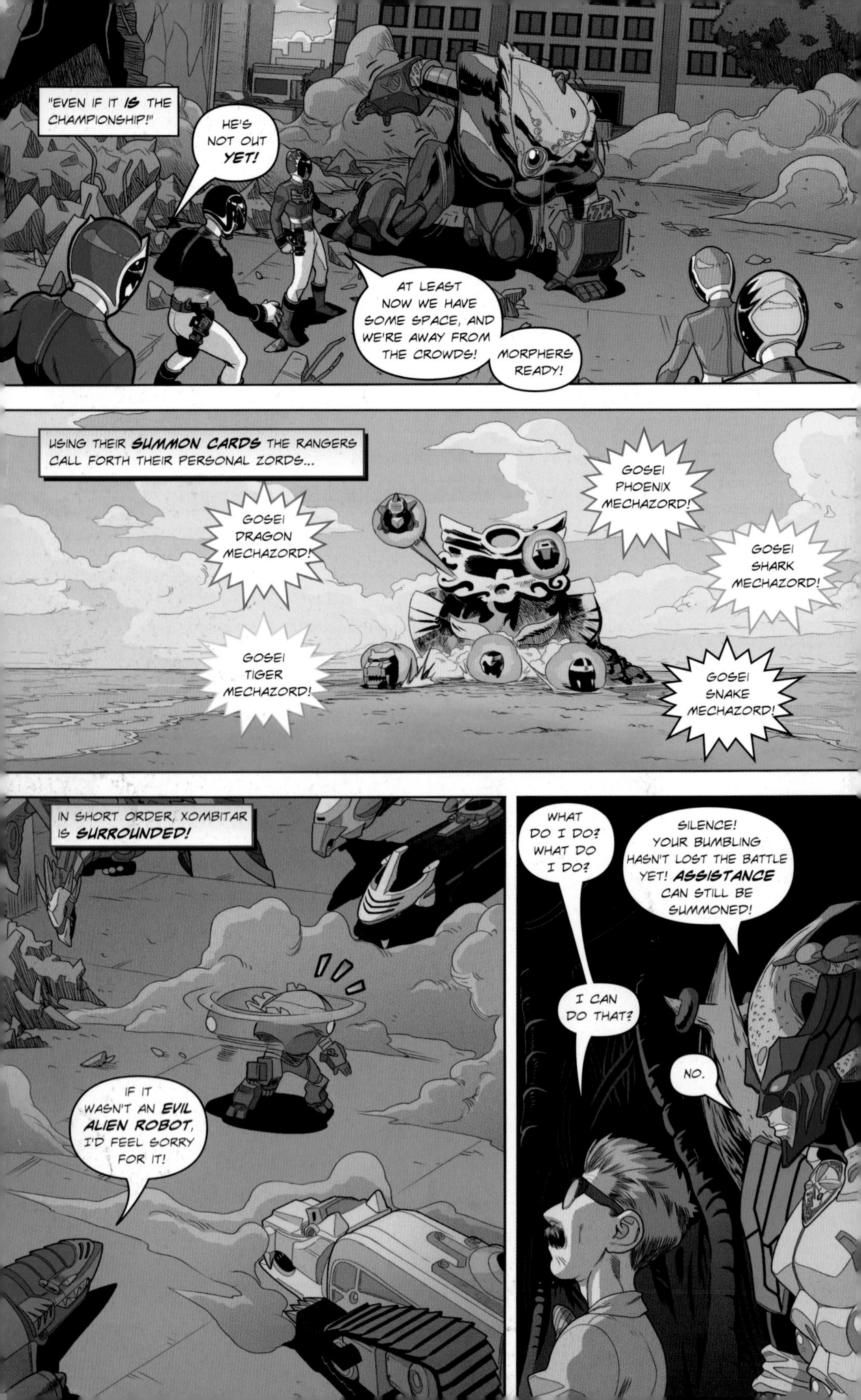
"EVEN IF IT IS THE CHAMPIONSHIP!"
HE'S NOT OUT YET!
AT LEAST NOW WE HAVE SOME SPACE, AND WE'RE AWAY FROM THE CROWDS!
MORPHERS READY!
USING THEIR SUMMON CARDS THE RANGERS CALL FORTH THEIR PERSONAL ZORDS...
GOSEI DRAGON MECHAZORD!
GOSEI PHOENIX MECHAZORD!
GOSEI SHARK MECHAZORD!
GOSEI TIGER MECHAZORD!
GOSEI SNAKE MECHAZORD!
IN SHORT ORDER, XOMBITAR IS SURROUNDED!
IF IT WASN'T AN EVIL ALIEN ROBOT, I'D FEEL SORRY FOR IT!
WHAT DO I DO? WHAT DO I DO?
SILENCE! YOUR BUMBLING HASN'T LOST THE BATTLE YET! ASSISTANCE CAN STILL BE SUMMONED!
I CAN DO THAT?
NO.

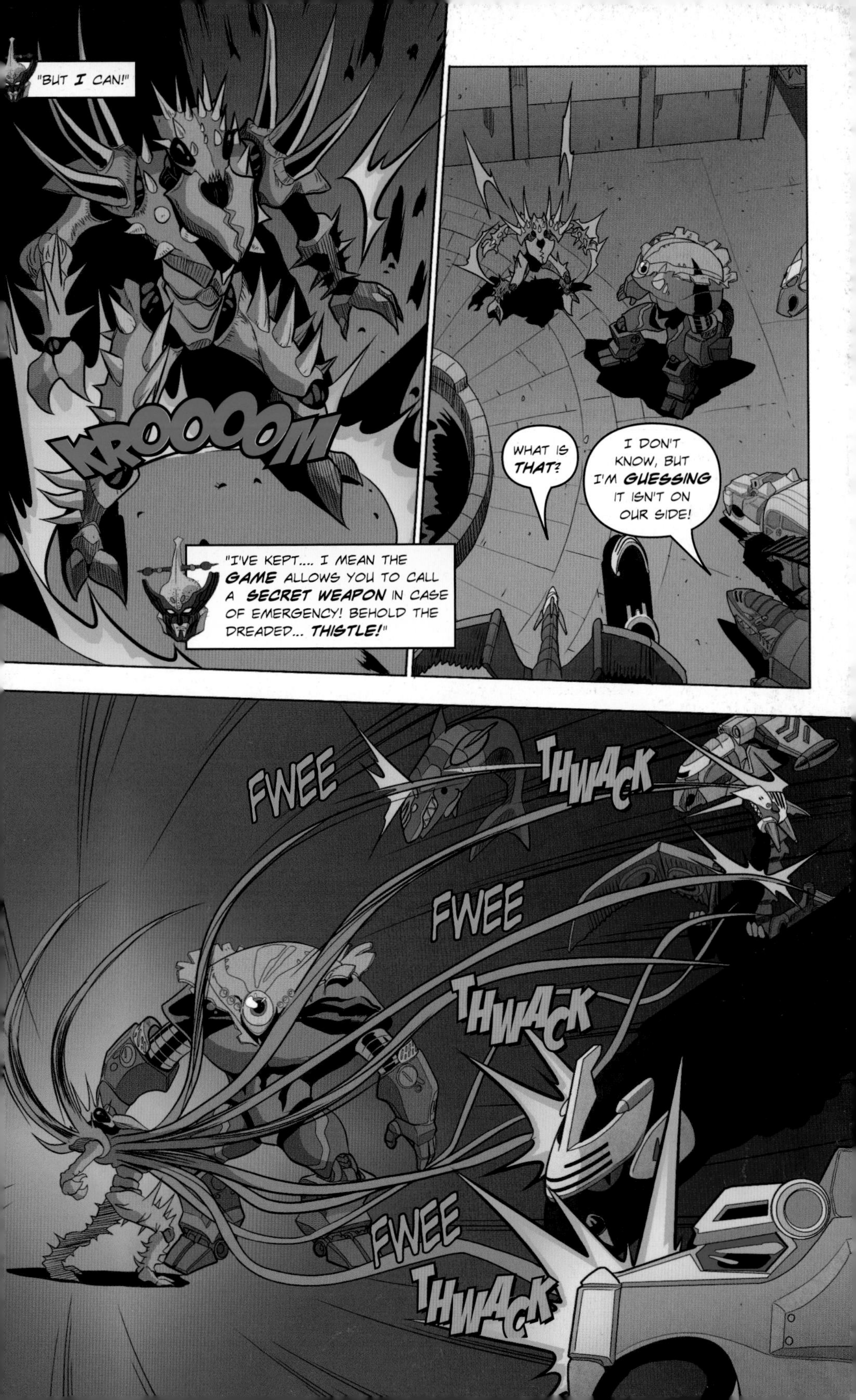
"BUT I CAN!"
KROOOOM
"I'VE KEPT.... I MEAN THE GAME ALLOWS YOU TO CALL A SECRET WEAPON IN CASE OF EMERGENCY! BEHOLD THE DREADED... THISTLE!"
WHAT IS THAT?
I DON'T KNOW, BUT I'M GUESSING IT ISN'T ON OUR SIDE!
FWEE
THWACK
FWEE
THWACK
FWEE
THWACK

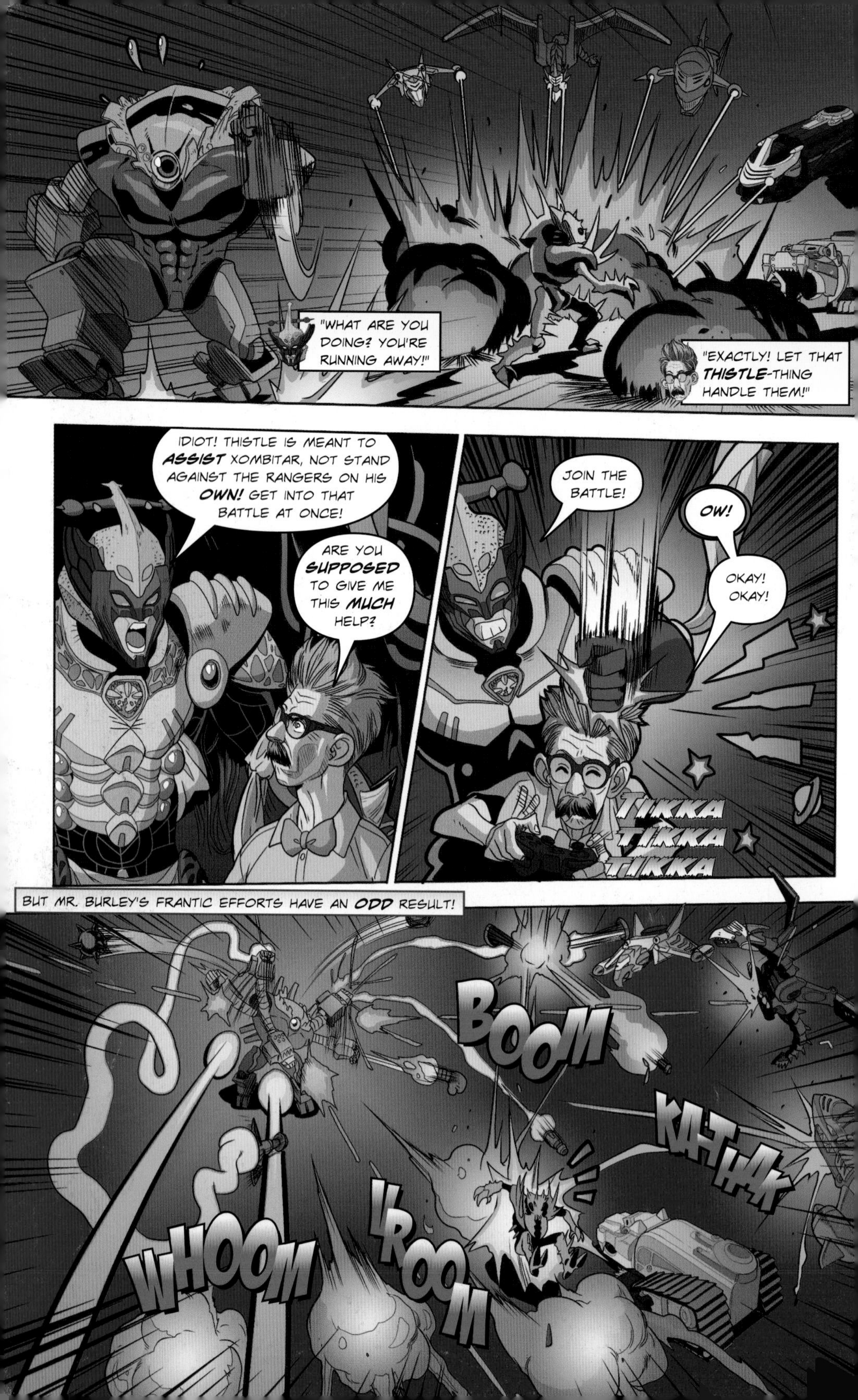
"WHAT ARE YOU DOING? YOU'RE RUNNING AWAY!"
"EXACTLY! LET THAT THISTLE-THING HANDLE THEM!"
IDIOT! THISTLE IS MEANT TO ASSIST XOMBITAR, NOT STAND AGAINST THE RANGERS ON HIS OWN! GET INTO THAT BATTLE AT ONCE!
ARE YOU SUPPOSED TO GIVE ME THIS MUCH HELP?
JOIN THE BATTLE!
OW!
OKAY! OKAY!
TIKKA TIKKA TIKKA
BUT MR. BURLEY'S FRANTIC EFFORTS HAVE AN ODD RESULT!
BOOM
KA-THAK
VROOM
WHOOM

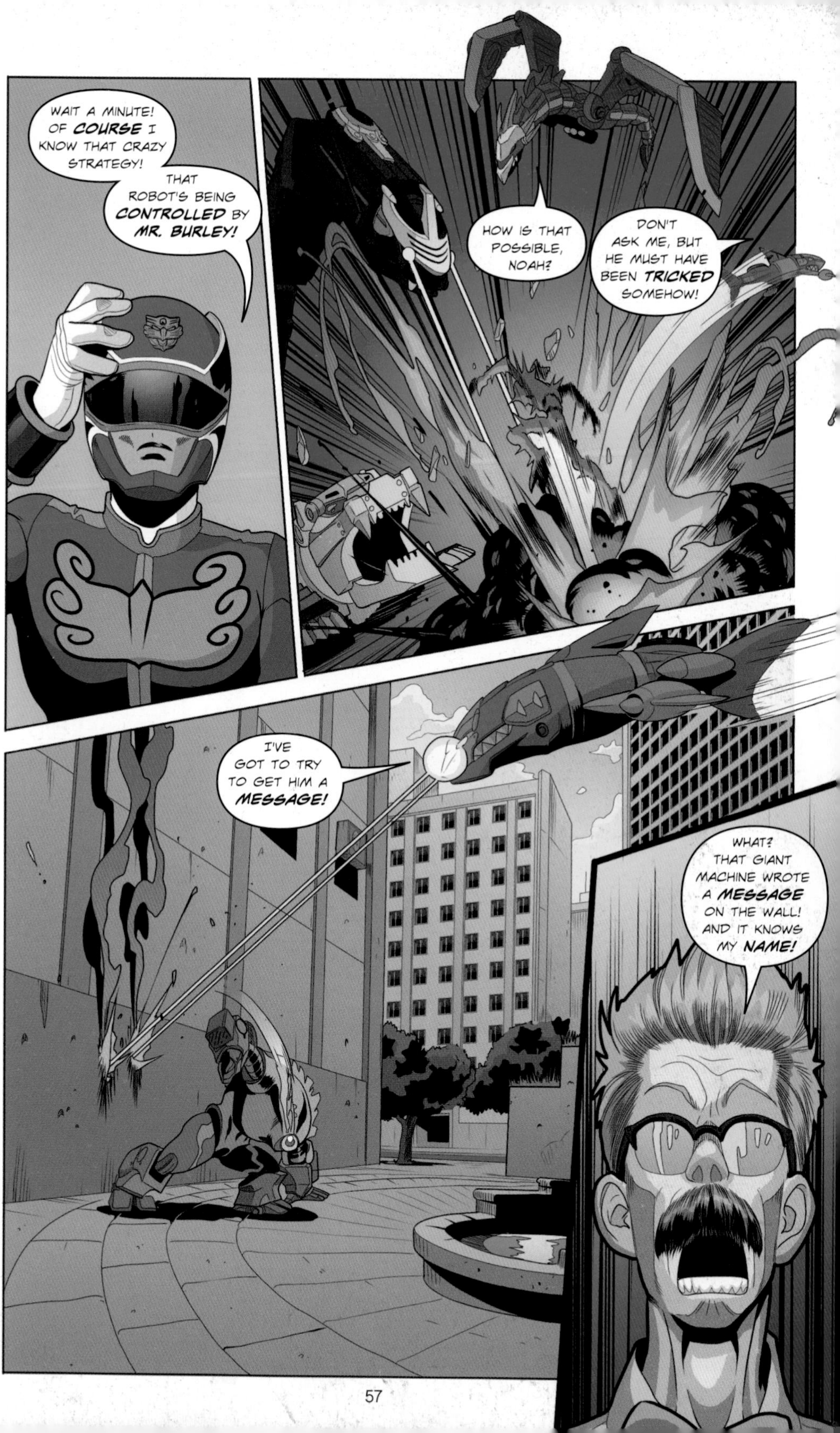
WAIT A MINUTE! OF COURSE I KNOW THAT CRAZY STRATEGY!
THAT ROBOT'S BEING CONTROLLED BY MR. BURLEY!
HOW IS THAT POSSIBLE, NOAH?
DON'T ASK ME, BUT HE MUST HAVE BEEN TRICKED SOMEHOW!
I'VE GOT TO TRY TO GET HIM A MESSAGE!
WHAT? THAT GIANT MACHINE WROTE A MESSAGE ON THE WALL! AND IT KNOWS MY NAME!

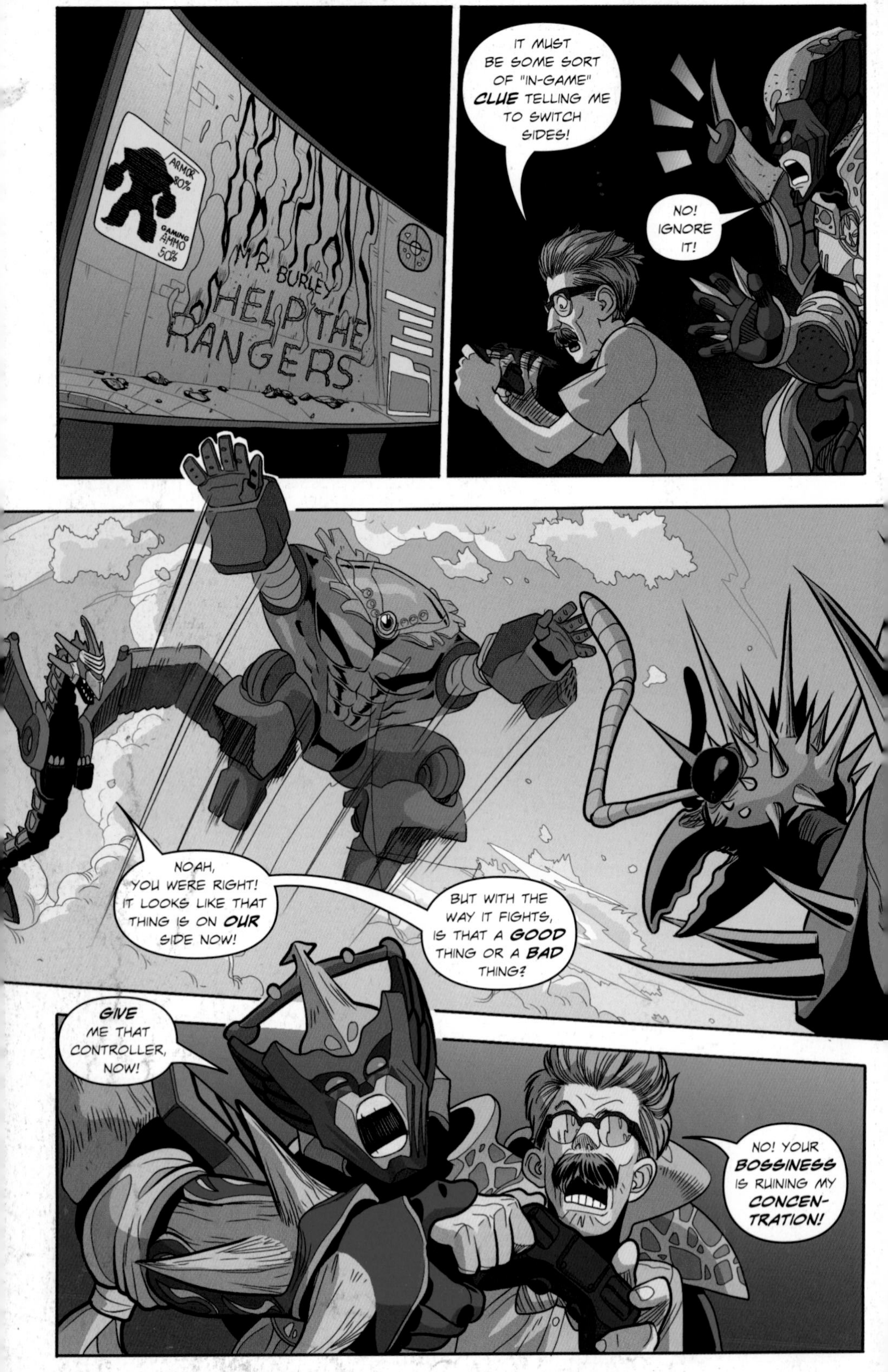
ARMOR 80%
GAMING AMMO 50%
MR. BURLEY
HELP THE RANGERS
IT MUST BE SOME SORT OF "IN-GAME" CLUE TELLING ME TO SWITCH SIDES!
NO! IGNORE IT!
NOAH, YOU WERE RIGHT! IT LOOKS LIKE THAT THING IS ON OUR SIDE NOW!
BUT WITH THE WAY IT FIGHTS, IS THAT A GOOD THING OR A BAD THING?
GIVE ME THAT CONTROLLER, NOW!
NO! YOUR BOSSINESS IS RUINING MY CONCEN-TRATION!

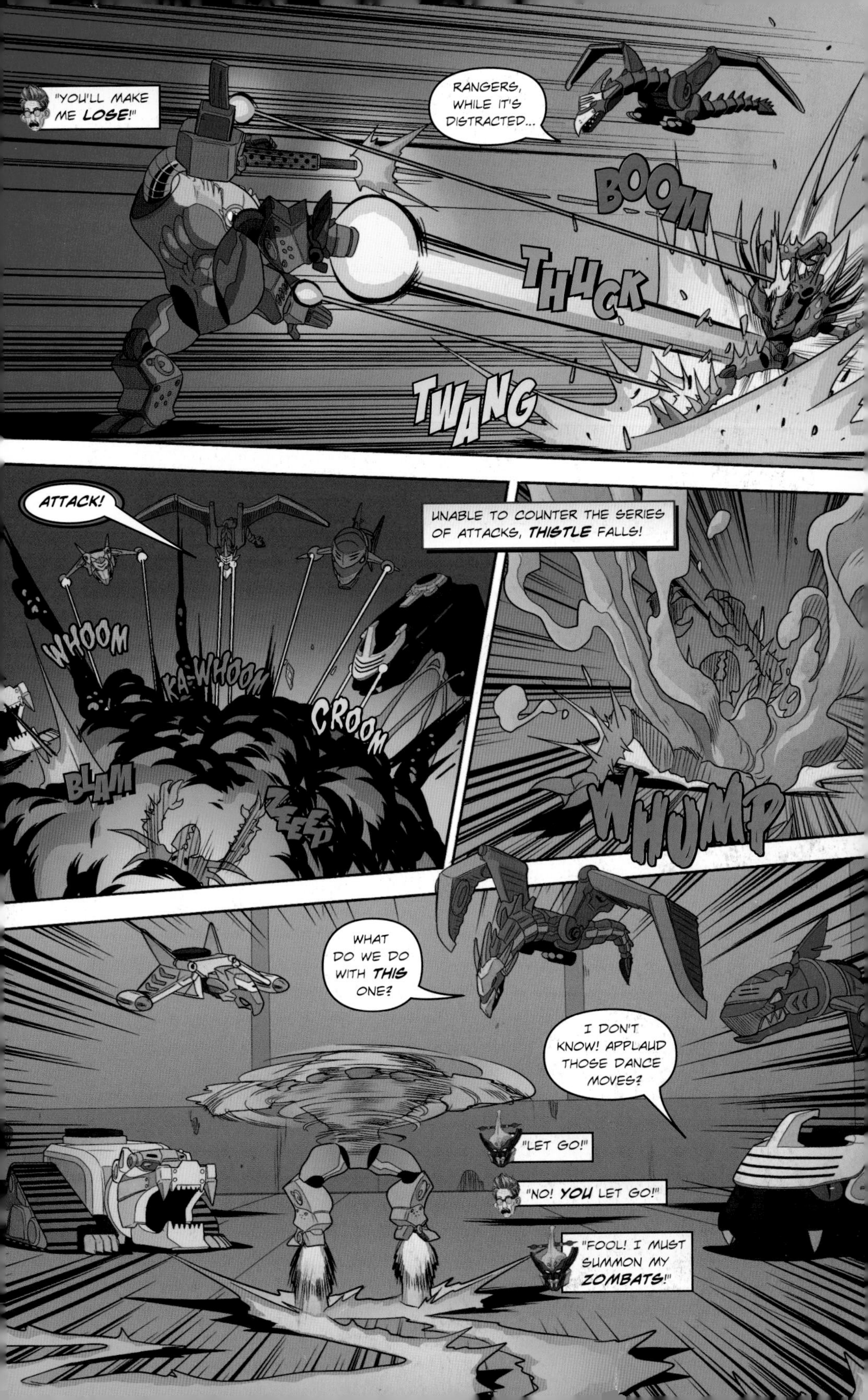

"YOU'LL MAKE ME LOSE!"
RANGERS, WHILE IT'S DISTRACTED...
BOOM
THUCK
TWANG
ATTACK!
WHOOM
KA-WHOOM
CROOM
BLAM
ZEEEP
UNABLE TO COUNTER THE SERIES OF ATTACKS, THISTLE FALLS!
WHUMP
WHAT DO WE DO WITH THIS ONE?
I DON'T KNOW! APPLAUD THOSE DANCE MOVES?
"LET GO!"
"NO! YOU LET GO!"
"FOOL! I MUST SUMMON MY ZOMBATS!"

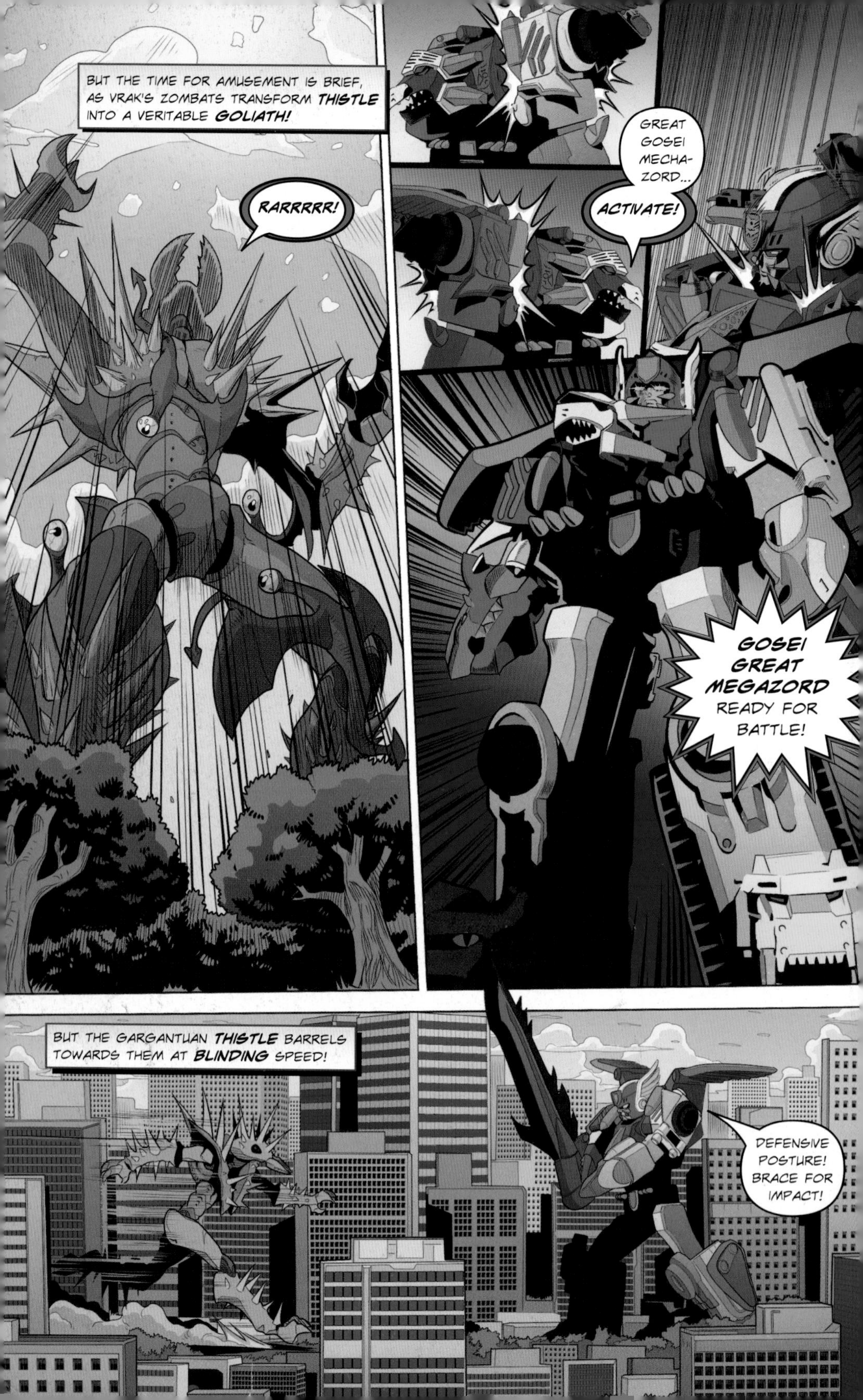
BUT THE TIME FOR AMUSEMENT IS BRIEF, AS VRAK'S ZOMBATS TRANSFORM **THISTLE** INTO A VERITABLE **GOLIATH!**
RARRRRR!
GREAT GOSEI MECHA-ZORD...
ACTIVATE!
GOSEI GREAT MEGAZORD READY FOR BATTLE!
BUT THE GARGANTUAN **THISTLE** BARRELS TOWARDS THEM AT **BLINDING** SPEED!
DEFENSIVE POSTURE! BRACE FOR IMPACT!

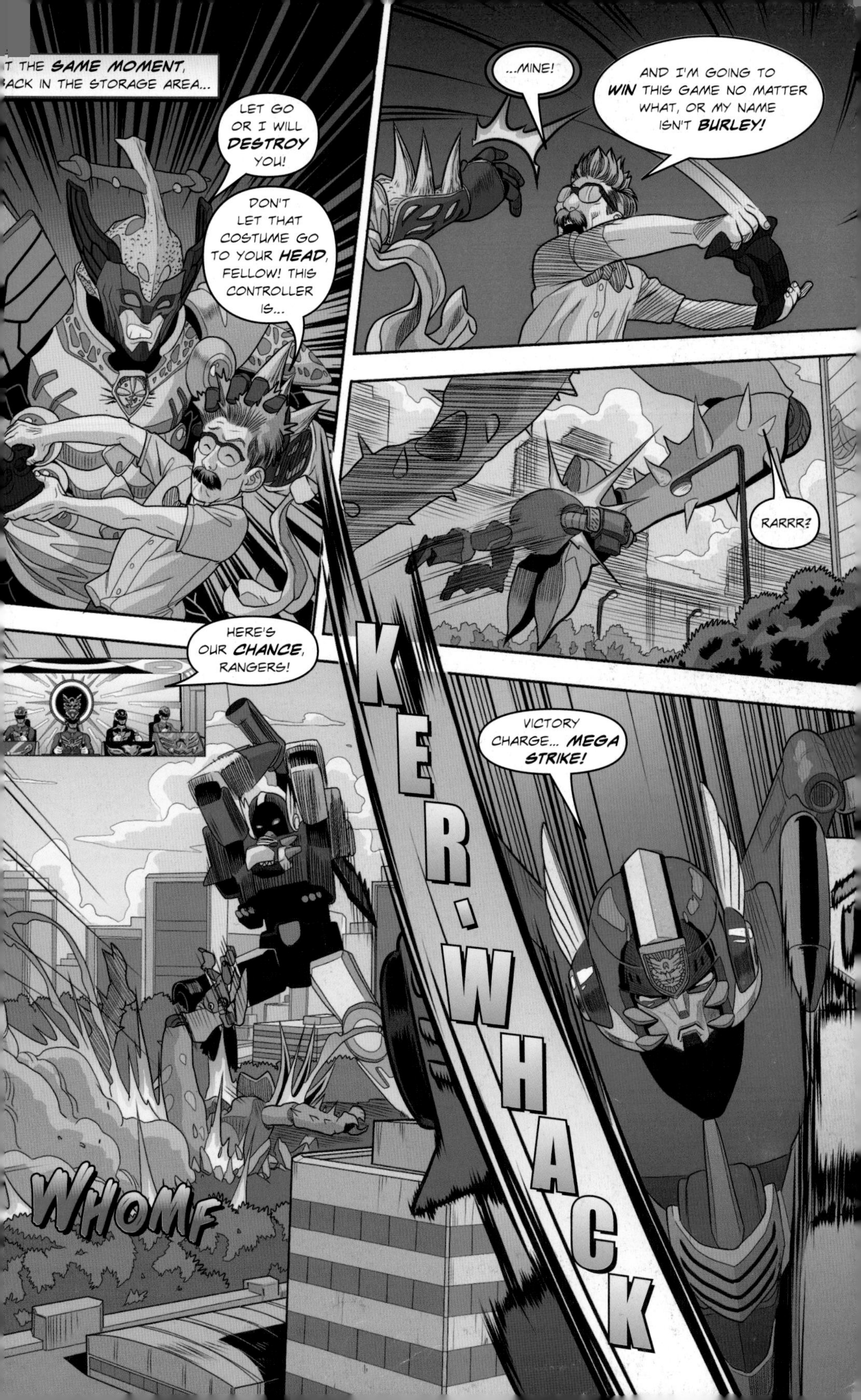
T THE SAME MOMENT, ACK IN THE STORAGE AREA...
LET GO OR I WILL DESTROY YOU!
DON'T LET THAT COSTUME GO TO YOUR HEAD, FELLOW! THIS CONTROLLER IS...
...MINE!
AND I'M GOING TO WIN THIS GAME NO MATTER WHAT, OR MY NAME ISN'T BURLEY!
RARRR?
HERE'S OUR CHANCE, RANGERS!
VICTORY CHARGE... MEGA STRIKE!
KER-WHACK
WHOMF

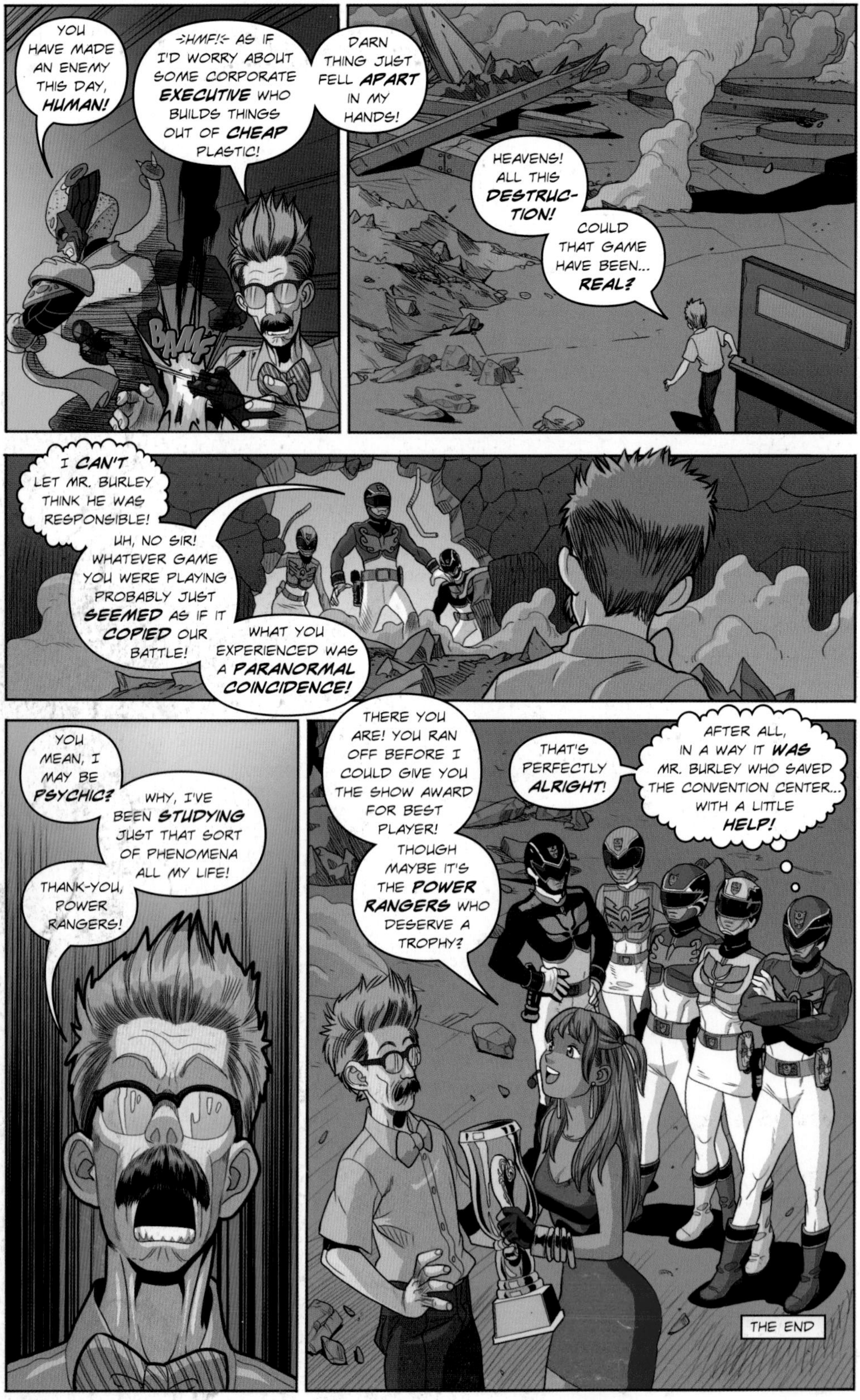
YOU HAVE MADE AN ENEMY THIS DAY, HUMAN!
>HMF!< AS IF I'D WORRY ABOUT SOME CORPORATE EXECUTIVE WHO BUILDS THINGS OUT OF CHEAP PLASTIC!
BAMF
DARN THING JUST FELL APART IN MY HANDS!
HEAVENS! ALL THIS DESTRUCTION!
COULD THAT GAME HAVE BEEN... REAL?
I CAN'T LET MR. BURLEY THINK HE WAS RESPONSIBLE!
UH, NO SIR! WHATEVER GAME YOU WERE PLAYING PROBABLY JUST SEEMED AS IF IT COPIED OUR BATTLE!
WHAT YOU EXPERIENCED WAS A PARANORMAL COINCIDENCE!
YOU MEAN, I MAY BE PSYCHIC?
WHY, I'VE BEEN STUDYING JUST THAT SORT OF PHENOMENA ALL MY LIFE!
THANK-YOU, POWER RANGERS!
THERE YOU ARE! YOU RAN OFF BEFORE I COULD GIVE YOU THE SHOW AWARD FOR BEST PLAYER!
THOUGH MAYBE IT'S THE POWER RANGERS WHO DESERVE A TROPHY?
THAT'S PERFECTLY ALRIGHT!
AFTER ALL, IN A WAY IT WAS MR. BURLEY WHO SAVED THE CONVENTION CENTER... WITH A LITTLE HELP!
THE END